SAVAGE DINOSAURS OF SOUTH DAKOTA

"Our teacher read KREEPY KLOWNS OF KALAMAZOO to us, and it was great. Everyone in my class is in love with your books!"

-Payton K., Age 10, Michigan

"How come you always end every chapter at a good part? It drives me crazy because I have to keep reading to find out what happened!"

-Shannon L., Age 12, Colorado

"My family and I went to Chillermania and you were there with all three of your dogs! It was the best day of my life!"

-Michael R., Age 10, Michigan

"I just started reading your books and I love them! I'm going to read your whole series!"

-Sandra B., Age 9, Mississippi

"I read your books under the covers with a flashlight every night. They give me nightmares, but I love every book!"

-Robbie H., age 10, Oregon

"I told my brother I was going to send in my Chiller Blurb and tell you how much I love your books, but he says that you won't print it. Will you print my Chiller Blurb to prove my brother wrong? P.S: He loves your books just as much as I do."

-Garrett G., age 11, Arizona

"You came to our school last year and were really funny! Everyone in our school wants you to come back!"

-Maria F., age 8, Delaware

"I got five of your books for my birthday, and they were all autographed by you! Thank you so much! It was the best birthday gift EVER!"

-Paul D, age 10, North Dakota

"I can't wait to read OGRES OF OHIO! That's where I live! My dad thinks the title is funny, and he says that he's the REAL Ogre of Ohio!"

-Erin T., age 11, Ohio

"You are my favorite author! I can't believe you've written so many books! Do you wear those creepy glasses when you write your books? Do they help you make your books even scarier?"

-Brad S., age 10, South Carolina

"I just found out that you're going to write a book for every state! How long is it going to take you to do that? Please hurry up, because I can't wait to read all of them!"

-Robyn W., age 13, Maine

Got something cool to say about Johnathan Rand's books? Let us know, and we might publish it right here! Send your short blurb to:

**Chiller Blurbs
281 Cool Blurbs Ave.
Topinabee, MI 49791**

AMERICAN CHILLERS

AMERICA'S #1 SERIES FOR MAXIMUM CHILLS!

#34: Savage Dinosaurs of South Dakota

Johnathan Rand

An AudioCraft Publishing, Inc. book

This book is a work of fiction. Names, places, characters and incidents are used fictitiously, or are products of the author's very active imagination.

Book storage and warehouses provided by Chillermania!©
Indian River, Michigan

American Chillers #34: Savage Dinosaurs of South Dakota
ISBN 13-digit: 978-1-893699-59-5

Librarians/Media Specialists:
PCIP/MARC records available **free of charge** at
www.americanchillers.com

Cover illustration by Dwayne Harris
Cover layout and design by Sue Harring

Printed in USA

Savage
Dinosaurs
of
South
Dakota

VISIT CHILLERMANIA!

WORLD HEADQUARTERS FOR BOOKS BY JOHNATHAN RAND!

CHILLERMANIA!

**I-75 Exit 313
then south
1 mile!**

Visit the HOME for books by Johnathan Rand! Featuring books, hats, shirts, bookmarks and other cool stuff not available anywhere else in the world! Plus, watch the American Chillers website for news of special events and signings at *CHILLERMANIA!* with author Johnathan Rand! Located in northern lower Michigan, on I-75! Take exit 313 . . . then south 1 mile! For more info, call (231) 238-0338. And be afraid! Be veeeery afraaaaaaiiiid . . . .

1

"Hey, Autumn!"

I turned when I heard my name, already recognizing the voice and knowing who it was: Brady Vanguard, a friend I'd met only a few months before. He and his family moved into the house across the street from ours, and he's in fifth grade, the same grade as me. Like me, he also has dark hair, and we are about the same height.

We like a lot of the same things, too, especially when it comes to food. My favorite food in the whole world is pizza, and so is his. He also loves ice cream, and so do I. We both like school, but we don't like homework. And we both love the movies.

And something we're both fascinated with is dinosaurs. As a matter of fact, that's how we got to know each other. In class one day, he saw a dinosaur book on my desk.

"That looks like a cool book," he said.

"Do you want to take a look at it?" I asked.

His eyes lit up. "I'd love to," he said.

I handed the book to Brady, and he flipped through it.

"These drawings and paintings are really awesome," he said.

"There's a ton of information in there, too," I said. "You can borrow it, if you want. My parents got it for me as a birthday gift. I've already read it once, but I carry it around with me because I like looking at the pictures."

Brady looked at me. "Really? You'd let me borrow it?" he asked.

"Sure," I replied. "I mean, you just moved

into the house across the street from ours. If you don't give it back, I know where to find you." I smiled, and Brady smiled back.

"Thanks," he said. "I'll give it back, I promise."

Ever since, we've been good friends. We worked together on a school project where we had to make dioramas. Our diorama featured dinosaurs, specifically, dinosaurs from the Mesozoic era. We worked on that project a lot: before school, during school, and even after school. Sometimes, we worked together on the weekends.

But our efforts paid off, and we both received an 'A' for our diorama.

Now, he was running up the street, shouting my name. When I turned, I saw him stop at the curb, look both ways, and begin to sprint across. He was carrying a newspaper, waving it in front of him.

"You're not going to believe this!" he said excitedly. "I don't even believe it myself!"

"What?" I asked.

By the time he reached me, he was out of breath. He'd probably been running a couple of blocks.

"This!" he said. "Check this out!" He handed me the newspaper.

I glanced at the headlines and looked at the picture. Then, I read the caption next to it.

My mouth fell open, and I think my heart skipped a beat.

"No way!" I said. "Is this for real?"

Brady bobbed his head. "As far as I can tell," he said. "It's not April first, so it's not an April Fool's joke. I think it's really going to happen."

I studied the article intently, and I couldn't believe what I was reading.

2

The newspaper article was about an eccentric inventor and entrepreneur who planned to build a dinosaur park in Rapid City, South Dakota, which is where we live. That's right: a dinosaur park. A couple of years ago, I saw a movie on television that was very similar. In the movie, the creatures were actual clones of dinosaurs, so they were alive and real.

But this inventor wasn't going to build a

park with *live* dinosaurs. All of the dinosaurs in his park were going to be mechanical, although he said they would look and move like real creatures. The difference being, of course, that the dinosaurs wouldn't need to eat food. They would all be powered by rechargeable batteries and programmed by computers.

"This sounds like something right out of a book," I said as I finished reading the article.

"Or a movie," Brady said. "Do you remember that movie about the live dinosaurs in the park?"

"I was just thinking of that while I read the article," I replied, and I pointed at the newspaper. "This park sounds a lot safer, being that the dinosaurs won't be alive."

"They sure look real," Brady said as he scanned the picture on the front page. It was a black-and-white photograph of two dinosaurs: a spinosaurus and a prosauropod. Although the pictures weren't in color, the dinosaurs appeared to be very real-looking.

My imagination went into overdrive. *A*

dinosaur park! I thought. *Right here, in Rapid City! How cool is that going to be?*

The inventor's name was Samuel Putnam, and he said he wanted to build the park for two reasons. First, to satisfy his love and fascination with dinosaurs. Second, he hoped to bring tourists to the area to enjoy the park and learn about the prehistoric lifestyles of the creatures. People could even get their pictures taken next to some of the most ferocious dinosaurs that ever walked the face of the Earth! He said that because the dinosaurs were controlled by computers and weren't alive, it would be a very safe family attraction.

And I believed him. Brady believed him. I think everyone who read the article probably believed him. Even Mr. Putnam himself believed that. I'm certain that, in his heart and in his mind, he really thought his dinosaur park would be safe for everyone.

He was dead wrong.

3

Construction on the dinosaur park began later that month. The location was an empty field not far from the city. The project wasn't expected to be complete for nearly a year, and that drove both Brady and me crazy. We were *so* anxious for the park to open. I even wrote a letter to Mr. Putnam himself, asking if Brady and I could buy the first tickets and be the first customers to visit the park. I went to the mailbox every day waiting for a return letter, but I never got one.

No matter. I figured Mr. Putnam was a very busy man, and he had to spend all of his time working on his park and his mechanical, computerized dinosaurs.

One day, there was an article in the newspaper about the project, giving an update on how it was coming along. Surprisingly, they were ahead of schedule, and Mr. Putnam said the park might open two months early, on April 24th instead of June 24th. I marked it on my calendar, and every day that went by, I placed an X on that particular date.

Brady and I became even more fascinated with dinosaurs. I think the dinosaur park helped fuel our imaginations even more. We wondered what kinds of dinosaurs Mr. Putnam had created for his park and if they would really look and move like actual dinosaurs.

"I think they'll look like the real thing," Brady said one day. "My dad says that scientists and inventors and engineers can do amazing things with robotics these days. That's pretty much what those dinosaurs are going to be: robots."

"I wonder if people will have to control them with a remote or if they'll be programmed by a computer?" I asked.

"They'll probably be programmed, each with its own individual computer," Brady speculated. "That way, he wouldn't have to hire very many workers. Just a couple of computer programmers would be all he would need."

"He might even do the computer programming himself," I said. "He sure sounds like a smart man."

"He's more than just smart," Brady said. "The guy's a genius. If he can figure out a way to make dinosaurs look and act like the real thing, like they really *are* alive, he's probably one of the smartest men on the planet."

The days passed slowly, and every day I put an X on my calendar. It drove me crazy. It was only March, and April 24th seemed a lifetime away.

But on the last day of March, something happened that was going to have a profound effect on my life.

It was Tuesday. I had walked to school, just like every other weekday. Brady and I walked home together, grumbling about the homework we'd been assigned. Not only homework, but math homework. The absolute worst kind of homework.

When we got to our houses, I said goodbye to Brady and walked to our mailbox. I flopped open the metal door and looked inside. There was only one letter there, which seemed a little odd. Usually, the mailbox is filled with letters. Sure, it's mostly junk mail, but it's a rare day when there's only one letter in the mailbox.

I reached in and pulled it out.

The envelope was addressed to me, which was strange. I hardly ever get any mail, except around my birthday.

And this was handwritten, too. Someone had sent me a handwritten letter.

Strange.

But even stranger—and much more exciting—was the name on the return address.

Mr. Samuel Putnam.

I tore open the envelope, and what I read made me more excited than anything else I'd ever experienced in my life.

4

Breathless, I read the letter.

Dear Ms. McLachlan,

I apologize for taking so long to reply to your letter, but I have been very busy working on my dinosaur park project and have had no time to respond to anyone.

I am thrilled that you are just as excited as I am about my new endeavor. I'm not sure if you saw the article in the newspaper or not, but construction of the park is ahead of schedule, and we will be opening in a few weeks, on April 24th. I will be hosting a grand opening with free food and beverages, tours, as well as souvenir prizes.

In your letter, you asked if you and your friend, Brady, could be the first to attend. It will be my pleasure to welcome both of you to my new park, and I will reserve the first two tickets in your names. When you get to the box office at the entrance of the park, simply tell them who you are, and they will take care of the rest.

I hope you enjoy my dinosaur park. I have been working toward this project since I was a little boy, and it is very rewarding and fulfilling to see my dream come true.

Very truly yours,
Samuel Putnam

I held the letter in my hands and realized that I was shaking. Then, I read it all over again.

I couldn't believe it! I had forgotten all about the letter I'd sent to Mr. Putnam, figuring he was too busy to get back to me. But he'd finally sent me a letter! Not only that, but he agreed to my request! Brady and I were going to be the first two kids to visit the dinosaur park!

Instead of going into my house, I ran to Brady's house. I pounded on the door so hard that they must've thought someone was trying to break in.

Mrs. Vanguard opened the door in surprise.

"Why, Autumn," she said. "What's the matter?"

"Mrs. Vanguard!" I blurted. "Is Brady home?" Which was a silly question. I'd watched him go into the house only moments before.

By then, Brady had reached the front door. His mother silently backed away, and Brady stepped forward, a puzzled expression on his face.

"What's up, Autumn?" he asked.

I waved the letter in front of his face. "This!" I said excitedly. "This is what's up!"

"What is it?" he asked as I handed him the letter.

"Read it!" I said.

Brady held the letter in front of his face, and I watched his lips move silently as he read. Slowly, his eyes widened. I could see the excitement growing on his face.

When he was finished, he lowered the letter.

"We're going to be the first people to visit the dinosaur park!" he shouted.

We started jumping up and down. Mrs. Vanguard reappeared in the living room, a look of surprise and curiosity on her face.

"What's all the ruckus about?" she asked.

"We're going to the dinosaur park, Mrs. Vanguard!" I said.

"Yeah, Mom!" Brady chimed. "Not only are we going to the dinosaur park, but Mr. Putnam says we can be the first two kids to visit!"

"Who is Mr. Putnam?" Mrs. Vanguard asked.

"He's the inventor who's building the park," I replied. "The dinosaur park has been a dream of his since he was little. I wrote him a letter, asking if Brady and I could be the first two kids to visit the park when it opens. I didn't get anything back from him, so I thought he forgot about my letter. Well, he didn't. I got this letter in the mail today."

Brady was still holding the letter, and he handed it to his mother. Mrs. Vanguard took it from him, and she read it. When she finished, she smiled and handed it back to me.

"It sounds like you two are in for an exciting day," Mrs. Vanguard said.

And she was right. Our visit to the dinosaur park would be filled with excitement.

But sometimes, excitement doesn't mean having fun. Sometimes, excitement can mean the opposite.

And sometimes, excitement can be disastrous . . . as we were about to find out.

5

If I had been impatient before, it was nothing compared to what I felt after receiving Mr. Putnam's letter. Each day, I couldn't wait until it was time to go to bed, because I knew I would wake up and it would be one day closer to the opening of the dinosaur park. I know it sounds kind of silly, but I was *so* excited, and I think a lot of kids my age would act the same way if they were excited about something.

And each day, I was careful to put another X on the calendar, noticing that the gap between that current day and the opening of the dinosaur park was getting smaller.

I even had dreams about it. In my dreams, I was transported back in time, watching dinosaurs in their habitat. It was so cool. When I woke up, I was mad, because I realized that it had been only a dream.

The night of April 23rd came. I climbed into bed at six o'clock, right after dinner. My parents and younger brother thought I was crazy, but I wanted to go to sleep so I could wake up early on the 24th. As it turned out, I had a hard time falling asleep, and I laid in bed until nearly eleven o'clock before I finally dozed off.

My alarm woke me at five in the morning. Normally, if I have to get up early, I stay in bed for a while, in a half-asleep daze.

Not today, though. I sprang out of bed, got dressed, and went into the kitchen. It was still dark outside, and my family was still sleeping. I quietly poured a bowl of cereal and ate at the table alone.

Today is the day! I thought. *It's finally here! The dinosaur park is opening today, and Brady and I are going to be the first to visit!*

When I finished breakfast, I washed the bowl and spoon, dried them, and put them away. Then, I returned to my room and walked to the window. I pulled back the drape a tiny bit and peeked outside. The surrounding houses were bathed in the salty blue glow of lights that seemed to hover above the shadowy street.

I let go of the drape, and it fell back into place. Then, I sat on my bed, glancing around my room, wondering what to do.

I looked at the clock.

5:25.

The dinosaur park was scheduled to open at noon, but Brady and I wanted to be there much earlier. Normally, for an event like this, my family would have gone with me. But my brother, Aaron, isn't the least bit interested in dinosaurs, which is a little strange. You would think an eight-year-old boy would be interested in something like that, but he's wasn't.

And both of my parents had to work that day, as did Brady's parents. It was a good thing the dinosaur park was only a couple of miles away, so we'd be able to ride our bikes there or walk if we really needed to. We wouldn't have to worry about getting a ride.

I passed the time in my room by flipping through a couple of dinosaur books and playing a few video games. After a while, I heard my little brother get up and turn on the television in the living room. A few minutes later, my parents got up, and I could hear them in the kitchen preparing breakfast and getting ready for work.

I left my bedroom and went down the hall.

"Hi, Mom," I said. "Good morning, Dad."

Both of my parents were still a little sleepy. "Good morning, Autumn," Mom replied. "How did you sleep?"

"Fine, after I was able to get to sleep," I said. "I was too excited."

"Today's the big day, huh?" Dad said.

I nodded and smiled. "Yep!" I said. "I can't wait! I've been waiting for this day for months and months!"

"Be sure to take your camera," Mom suggested. "Take lots of pictures."

"Oh, I will," I replied. "That's one thing I planned on."

Actually, I'd planned on several things. I'd planned on eating lunch in the park's dinosaur café. I'd planned on buying some souvenirs. I was certain the park would be selling T-shirts, and I planned on buying one of those, too.

The one thing I hadn't planned for?

Tragedy.

But nobody plans for tragedy. If you know tragedy is coming, you make plans to avoid it.

Unfortunately, for Brady and me, it was already too late for that.

Brady called me at eight o'clock.

"Are you ready?" he asked.

"I was ready back in December!" I said. "I've been ready since I woke up at five o'clock this morning!"

There really wasn't much that I needed to take with me, but I wore a small backpack, anyway. I put a couple of bottles of water in it, along with a banana, a fruit juice, and a candy bar.

It was a little chilly, so I wore a thick, hooded sweatshirt with pockets in the front. I put my digital camera and my change purse in the pockets.

My bike was in the garage, and I pushed it down the driveway. Brady was already waiting for me at the sidewalk. He, too, was wearing his backpack.

"Ready?"

I bobbed my head. "Like I told my mom: I've been waiting for this day for months and months."

We started out together, riding side-by-side along the sidewalk.

"My mom thinks we're crazy," Brady said as we rode through the chilly morning air.

"Why is that?" I asked.

"She says there's no need to get to the park early, because we're already guaranteed to be the first two kids in the park," he said.

"I don't care," I said. "I can't wait around the house any longer. It's driving me crazy. If we get there early, maybe we'll find something to do. Maybe the souvenir shop will be open."

"Maybe we'll have the chance to meet Mr. Putnam," Brady said.

"I hope so," I said. "I want to thank him for sending me the letter and letting us be the first kids in the park."

We continued on our bikes, chatting excitedly, talking about the park and what it would be like. I had saved the newspaper articles and read them over and over again. I knew a lot about the park, even though it hadn't opened yet.

Finally, after about a half hour of pedaling and winding around and through city streets and sidewalks, we made a final turn. The dinosaur park came into view in the distance.

The scene was so stunning and impressive that we had to stop our bikes and stare.

"Holy cow," Brady said in amazement.

"The place is huge," I said.

The dinosaur park had been built in an open field. There were no other buildings or structures near it, except for a small mobile home that probably served as a tool or maintenance shed, and there was yet another windowless building behind it. Other than that, the dinosaur park sat alone on a flat plane, with the foothills of the mountains in the distance behind it.

From the outside, the park looked like a fortress. The only things we could see were high brick walls reaching three stories into the air. Dozens of dinosaur statues sat on top of the walls, staring down as if they were guarding the facility. Directly in front of the park was a wide, open parking lot containing about a dozen vehicles.

"I guess I didn't realize how big the place was going to be," Brady said.

"Well," I said, "the newspaper article said that there would be nearly two hundred different dinosaurs. I would imagine they would need a lot of space to roam, even if they are mechanical."

We continued pedaling, but we couldn't take our eyes off the enormous structure before us. The entrance to the park was as impressive as the structure itself. It had two enormous doors almost as tall as the walls. Above it was a colorful sign depicting a dinosaur scene. It read:

WELCOME TO PUTNAM'S DINOSAUR PARK!
A JOURNEY BACK IN TIME FOR THE WHOLE FAMILY!

Because we were so early, there wasn't anyone around. I was a little disappointed, because I was hoping there might be something else to see. Apparently, we were going to have to wait until noon for the doors to open.

"Hey," Brady said. "Let's kill some time and ride around the outside of the place."

"Okay," I said. "But I was really hoping there would be more going on. I guess it's still too early."

"Who cares?" Brady said. "It's exciting just to be here."

We rode our bikes around the north side of the building. The ground was hard-packed dirt with a few weeds and grass patches. In some places, the dirt had been disturbed by the tires of large vehicles. We saw two normal-sized doors, each with signs that read *Employees Only*.

"Not much to see here," I said.

Then, we reached the back of the park where I saw something that made me hit the brakes and skid to a sudden stop. Brady saw what I was looking at, and stopped.

"Is that what I think it is?" he asked.

"If you're seeing a dinosaur, then the answer is yes," I replied.

We were too far away to tell exactly what kind of dinosaur it was, but it was huge. It stood on its hind legs, and its head wavered about, cocking to the left and to the right. Then, he appeared to sniff the air before once again turning his enormous head from side to side, as if he were listening to something.

"What's he doing *outside* of the park?" Brady asked.

"I have no idea," I said, shaking my head.

Near the dinosaur, we saw the figure of a man standing, and I assumed it was probably an employee of the park. Maybe it was Mr. Putnam himself.

But in the next moment, my fascination

turned to stunned horror. In one lightning-fast motion, the dinosaur turned toward the man, opened his powerful jaws, leaned forward, and took him in his mouth!

7

I drew a sudden, deep breath.

"Oh, no!" I said, barely able to spit out the words.

"That dinosaur is eating that guy!" Brady exclaimed.

We could only watch, terrified, as the dinosaur chewed up the helpless man and swallowed him. The entire incident had taken less than fifteen seconds.

"We've got to tell someone!" I said. "Something's gone horribly wrong!"

We quickly turned our bikes around and began pedaling, stopping at one of the first doors we came to, one of the doors with the sign that read *Employees Only*.

I stopped, leapt off my bike, ran to the door, and pounded on it.

"Is there anybody there?" I said loudly. I continued pounding. "Hello? Is anyone around?"

"Let's try the other door," Brady said.

I returned to my bicycle, and we continued to the next door. Again, I pounded, but there was no response.

"What do we do?" Brady asked.

"Let's go to the police," I said. "We've got to let them know that something is wrong at the park. Even if that's a mechanical dinosaur, he ate a man! There's no telling what it might do!"

We were about to pedal away when the door suddenly opened, taking us both by surprise. An older man appeared. He was well-dressed, wearing black pants, a white dress shirt, and a colorful tie with dinosaurs on it. His hair was the color of steel, and he wore glasses with very thick lenses.

"May I help you?" he asked. He seemed a little confused, and I'm sure he hadn't expected someone to be pounding on the door.

"One of the dinosaurs is loose out back!" I shouted, pointing. "We watched him eat a man!"

"Yeah!" Brady said. "He chewed him up, and everything! We saw it with our own eyes!"

The man frowned, and the lines on his forehead deepened. He looked puzzled.

Then, his eyes lit up and a smile formed.

"Oh, that," he said with a careless wave of his bony hand. "That's nothing to worry about."

"Nothing to worry about?!?!" I said. "One of those dinosaurs just killed somebody!"

The man shook his head and laughed.

"No," he said, "that's not what happened. You see, that dinosaur is part of one of our demonstrations. The man you saw being eaten wasn't a real man. It was only a dummy. The demonstration shows how easy it would be for that kind of dinosaur to attack an average-sized human being."

"Oh, gross," Brady said.

Again, the man shook his head. "Actually, it's not gross at all. There's no blood, and the man is actually made out of rubber. The dinosaur appears to chew him up and swallow him, because that's what his computer is programmed to do. It's a powerful demonstration, and quite educational, although I can see where it might upset some of our younger visitors . . . especially if they think the dinosaur is eating a real, live human."

"How come he's outside?" Brady asked. "How come he's not in the park?"

"We moved him outside for some final testing, because his demonstration area inside the park needed some work. There was an electrical malfunction in his arena, and it's being worked on by my employees right now. I wanted to run a couple more tests on the dinosaur before we open the park later today, and it was easier to move the robot to the back, outside of the park where there is more room. Really, there's nothing to worry about."

I suddenly felt very silly. Brady and I had actually thought the mechanical dinosaur had eaten a live human being! What a relief to find out that we were wrong.

The man spoke again. This time, it was his turn to ask questions.

"What were you two doing behind the park, anyway?" he asked, glancing at Brady and then at me, where his eyes and focus remained.

"We got here early, because we're excited about the grand opening," I replied.

"Yeah," Brady chimed in. "We were just killing time, so we decided to ride our bicycles around the outside of the park."

"I wrote a letter to Mr. Putnam," I said. "He wrote me a letter back, saying that we could be the first two visitors to the park."

"Oh, he did, did he?" the man said with a smile.

I nodded. "Yes," I said. "I wrote him a letter months ago, but he didn't write me back, and I figured he forgot about it. But then, a few weeks ago, he wrote me a letter back."

While I spoke, the man's grin continued to widen.

"Wait a minute," I said. "You're not—"

The man nodded gently.

Brady spoke. "You mean you're—"

"Mr. Samuel Putnam," the man said as he bowed slightly. "At your service."

He stepped back and opened the door wider.

"Do come in," he said. "I've got a little time before things get really busy, and I can show you around a bit."

I looked at Brady, and he looked at me. We must've hesitated a little too long, because Mr. Putnam laughed.

"Don't worry," he said. "It's all right. Come in. Bring your bikes, and you can put them in the storage room where they'll be safe."

My heart was pounding as I slipped off of

my bicycle and pushed it through the doorway.

My dream was coming true, and it was better than ever. Not only did I get to visit a dinosaur park, not only did I get to be one of the very first visitors, but now I was getting my own private tour from the famous inventor himself, Mr. Samuel Putnam.

"I am never going to forget this day," Brady whispered in my ear as we leaned our bikes against an inside wall.

Brady was absolutely right. Neither one of us would forget that day . . . but it would be for all the wrong reasons.

8

The room we entered was dimly lit by a single bulb suspended from the ceiling. There were shelves on all of the walls and those contained boxes; nothing else.

"Just leave your bikes there, against the wall," Mr. Putnam said. "They'll be fine. No one comes into this room, anyway."

Brady and I did as he asked, leaning our bikes against the wall. I slipped off my backpack and hung it on the seat, and Brady did the same.

Mr. Putnam closed and locked the door and led us through the room to yet another door. He opened it, and we followed him down a long, carpeted hallway.

"I can't believe this is happening!" I whispered to Brady.

"We are the luckiest kids in Rapid City," he whispered back. *"We're getting a private tour from the famous inventor himself!"*

Mr. Putnam continued on, and we walked several steps behind him. For an older guy, he was quite nimble and quick on his feet.

"I think we'll start with the command control center," he said, turning his head slightly to address us. "That's about as good a place as any to begin."

All sorts of questions buzzed in my head, but I decided to keep quiet for the time being. I didn't want to say anything that sounded silly. Besides, during our tour, Mr. Putnam would probably answer a lot of my questions before I even asked them.

"Here we are," he said, and he stopped before a large metal door. The sign on it read *Danger - Employees Only.*

Mr. Putnam saw me staring at the sign.

"Oh, don't worry," he said. "There really isn't any danger. It's just that I don't want any unauthorized people to be wandering through the command control center. Only people who know what they're doing should be inside."

He pulled a plastic card from his pocket and waved it in front of a small panel next to the door. There was a loud click as the lock mechanism disengaged, and Mr. Putnam pushed open the door.

I wasn't sure what I had expected to see, but the room was nothing like I had envisioned.

For the most part, the floor was empty. Near the walls, however, there were dozens of computers and monitors. Above the computer monitors were large, flat screen televisions, each displaying a different scene. Each scene was of a different dinosaur in his environment. The dinosaurs were frozen, standing like statues. Plants grew up and around them, and there were numerous large rocks and various colors of sand.

"This is the park's closed-circuit monitoring system," Mr. Putnam explained. "There are cameras placed all around the inside of the park, allowing us to see most of the areas."

"How come the dinosaurs aren't moving?" Brady asked.

"Because the park isn't open yet," Mr. Putnam replied. "There's really no sense in having them move around while the park is closed."

That made sense. If the dinosaurs were powered by rechargeable batteries, it would probably be a waste to have them operating when it wasn't necessary.

I pointed to the plants displayed in one of the television screens. "I recognize those plants," I said. "I've seen them in some of my dinosaur books. How did you get them to grow?"

Mr. Putnam shook his head. "They don't

grow," he said. "They're synthetic. They're made of a combination of plastic and fiberglass. When we go out there, I'll give you a chance to touch some of the leaves. They actually look and feel like real plants."

"Man," Brady said as he shook his head. "You really thought of everything."

Mr. Putnam laughed. "You haven't seen anything yet," he said. "Watch this."

He walked to one of the computers and tapped the keyboard. Above, one of the large, flat screen televisions blinked off. The screen went dark.

Suddenly, it was filled with another scene altogether. My jaw fell. I could only stare in amazement.

9

"You should see some movement in a moment," Mr. Putnam said.

On the screen were three large dinosaur eggs in what appeared to be a small cave. The eggs were slate gray with a few dark speckles. While we watched, they began to rock slightly.

"Dinosaur eggs?" Brady asked.

Mr. Putnam nodded. "I thought it would be great to show people how dinosaurs actually hatched," he said. "Keep watching."

We remained glued to the screen as the eggs began to tremble more and more. Finally, a crack appeared in one of the eggs, and something moved inside. Soon, the shell cracked in two pieces, and a small, groggy dinosaur emerged. Its eyes were barely open, and it had difficulty walking. The other two eggs hatched, bringing forth two more tiny dinosaurs. The young creatures quickly adjusted to their new environment, to their new life outside of the egg, and were scampering playfully all around the cave.

"And those things are mechanical?" I asked.

Mr. Putnam nodded. "Yes," he answered. "All of the dinosaurs are robots. When you get a chance to see the inside of one, which you will soon, you will see that they are all electronic."

"But what about their skin?" Brady asked.

"Yeah," I said. "It looks so real."

"It's the same material that the plant leaves are made out of," Mr. Putnam said, "although the makeup is a little bit different. Each dinosaur skin has a different construction, containing different elements, depending on what look I was trying to achieve. My goal was to make each dinosaur look as real as possible, and the skin was a very important part of the development of each creature."

Brady whistled. "Wow," he said. "How much did all of this cost?"

Again, Mr. Putnam laughed. It was an easy, comfortable laugh, and I liked him more and more. I'd heard he was supposed to be kind of strange and eccentric, but I found him to be quite kind and very polite.

"I'm not going to go into the exact figures," he said, "but you might say that I have been working my entire life to earn enough money for this project. I've been very fortunate to create some very profitable inventions over the years, which brought me a considerable amount of money. Enough to make my dream of owning a dinosaur park a reality. I'm living proof that if you work hard and work smart, your dreams can come true."

I couldn't take my eyes off the baby dinosaurs on the television screen. They looked so real that it was hard to believe they were actually battery-powered robots with electronics in their bodies. They even moved like real dinosaurs. Not that I had seen any *real* dinosaurs move, of course, but they just seemed so lifelike. Once word got out, I knew people would be coming from all across the country to Putnam's Dinosaur Park.

Suddenly, the room was filled with a shrill, high-pitched siren. On the wall above one of the large, flat screen televisions, a red light the size of a softball began flashing. Beneath it, on the television screen, the word *WARNING* appeared in red letters. Like the red light, it, too, was blinking.

Mr. Putnam looked alarmed.

"Uh-oh," he said. "That's not good. That's not good at all."

The alarm continued to scream in my ears, and Mr. Putnam quickly got to work. He moved to a computer several feet away and began tapping furiously at the keyboard.

"What's wrong?" Brady asked. However, the alarm was so loud that I don't think Mr. Putnam heard the question. He remained focused on the computer screen in front of him, tapping away.

The alarm stopped ringing, and the red light

stopped blinking. The warning on the television screen disappeared.

"What happened?" I asked.

"No big deal, after all," he said. "There's a computer glitch somewhere that's causing a little trouble now and then. I think I've got it taken care of."

I looked up at the large, flat screen television, watching the small, newly-hatched baby dinosaurs scampering around in the cave. Once again, I found it hard to believe that they weren't real.

Mr. Putnam is a genius, I thought. *He's got to be one of the smartest guys on the planet.*

I glanced around at some of the other large screens. They displayed various dinosaurs, motionless and statue-like. Like the baby dinosaurs, they, too, looked unbelievably real.

"Will we be able to touch them?" Brady asked.

Mr. Putnam shook his head. "Not most of them, no," he replied. "Most of them are too big, and I can't allow the public to get close to them. However, there is a small part of the park that contains a few dinosaurs that don't move. It's actually a play area for the smaller children. Those dinosaurs are made just like the other ones in the park, except they have no electronic equipment inside."

"Do you mind if I take a couple of pictures of the command control center?" I asked.

"Not at all," was Mr. Putnam's reply.

I pulled my digital camera from the front pocket of my sweatshirt and took a couple of pictures.

"Brady," I said, "stand next to Mr. Putnam, and I'll take your picture."

Brady moved next to Mr. Putnam. They both were all smiles as I took a couple of pictures. Then, I gave the camera to Brady, and he took a picture of me next to Mr. Putnam.

"So," Mr. Putnam said, "this is pretty much it for the command control center. Let's move on, and I'll show you the laboratory where we actually create the dinosaurs."

We left the command control center and walked back into the hallway. Mr. Putnam walked and talked easily and freely. I could tell he was very proud of his creation, and for good reason. Not only that, he treated us like adults, very respectful and polite. He didn't talk down to us like some adults do.

Unfortunately, while we walked, none of us were aware that there was already a series of events taking place that would threaten to destroy Mr. Putnam's dinosaur park. Not only that, but soon, the entire city of Rapid City would be in danger of devastation and chaos on a catastrophic scale.

11

The electronics laboratory where the dinosaurs were created and built was unlike anything I'd ever seen in my life. It was the first place where we saw people, other than Mr. Putnam. They all wore the same clothing: black pants with white golf shirts that had the Putnam's Dinosaur Park logo embroidered on the left breast. There were about two dozen people in all, both men and women. A few of them wore long, white lab coats.

"This is where we construct the dinosaurs," Mr. Putnam explained. "And if there's a problem with any of them, this is where we'll bring them for repairs."

He stopped speaking, allowing us to look around and take in everything we were seeing.

The room had high ceilings, and it was much bigger than the command control center. In fact, it was almost as big as our school gymnasium. Long tables were lined up in rows throughout the entire area, creating aisles for the men and women to walk up and down. Some of the tables were small, and some were very large. On one of these larger tables was an enormous stegosaurus. It lay on its side, and its stomach was open. Inside the creature was a network of wires and thin cables, all sorts of electronic gadgetry and gizmos that I knew nothing about. In fact, the whole concept of electricity mystified me. I really didn't understand how it worked other than when I flipped a switch in my bedroom, a light came on. That same electricity charged the battery for my digital camera.

I thought about the late Thomas Edison, the inventor of the electric lightbulb, along with hundreds and hundreds of other cool inventions.

Imagine what he would think if he could see how powerful electricity has become, I thought. *I wonder if he ever imagined that electricity would have so many uses, like bringing dinosaurs to life. I wonder if Thomas Edison knew how electricity would change the world.*

"Can we get a closer look at that stegosaurus?" Brady asked, pointing.

"Sure," Mr. Putnam said. "We're just doing a little rewiring on his circuitry."

Mr. Putnam began walking through the room, weaving around tables. We followed close behind. The men and women working in the room smiled and nodded as he passed. He acknowledged the silent greetings with his own nods and smiles.

"What was wrong with the stegosaurus?" I asked.

"I'm not really sure," Mr. Putnam replied.

"We were noticing some strange behavior in his presentation area. He was doing some things he wasn't originally programmed to do. I don't think it's a serious issue, though. After all, we're only human, and humans make mistakes now and then. We'll get him fixed."

I was starting to get a strange feeling about all of this. While I was still very excited to be given our own private tour of Putnam's Dinosaur Park, I began to get an uneasy flutter in my gut.

First, they're testing a dinosaur outside of the park because it wasn't working properly, I thought. *Then, we're in the command control center and an alarm goes off, and we still don't know what that was about. And a stegosaurus that is doing things that it wasn't programmed to do?*

It seemed to me like there were several problems that had occurred, each with their own degree of seriousness. The stegosaurus was a huge dinosaur. What if it malfunctioned when the park was filled with tourists? What if, all of sudden, it ran amok and couldn't be stopped?

Stop being silly, I told myself. *Mr. Putnam is a genius. He wouldn't allow something like that to happen. He's too smart, he's worked too hard, and he's thought of everything.*

Mr. Putnam also said that we're only human, and humans make mistakes . . . but I didn't remember that until later, after the horrifying carnage began.

12

I tried to push aside my uneasiness, but I couldn't. So, I simply tried to ignore it. I had been offered the opportunity of a lifetime, and I didn't want to waste my time thinking about bad things that probably wouldn't happen.

There was a man and a woman working on the stegosaurus. They spoke to Mr. Putnam, assuring him that the dinosaur had been repaired.

"There were a couple of problems," the

woman explained. "A couple of wires had been broken, probably due to the creature's own movements. This is something we'll have to take note of in the future, and make sure that we extend some of these wires a bit."

"What's the other problem?" Mr. Putnam asked.

This time the man spoke. "That's a more complicated issue," he said, scratching his head. "It was a problem with his programming, but we don't understand why. It was as if he was receiving commands from someplace other than the command control center. The problem seems to have fixed itself, although we don't know exactly why it occurred in the first place."

Mr. Putnam looked at his watch. "Well," he said, "you still have a little bit of time before the park is officially open. Run some more tests, but if the stegosaurus performs fine, wheel him back out into the park."

"Just how do you control the dinosaurs?" I asked. I knew that they were battery-powered, and

I knew that they were computer-guided, but I wasn't sure how they received commands.

"Each dinosaur is remotely controlled by a single computer in the command control center," Mr. Putnam explained. "There is a software program on the computer that's designed to control the motions of the dinosaur so that it mimics what we believe would be exactly how that particular creature would have moved. The commands are sent by a radio signal that is picked up by a receiver in each dinosaur."

"Kind of like a remote control car or airplane," Brady said.

Mr. Putnam nodded. "Exactly," he said. "Of course, our system is quite a bit more sophisticated. Remote control cars and airplanes only weigh a few pounds. Some of our dinosaurs weigh several *tons*. Speaking of which: how about we take a look at some of them in action, before the crowds arrive?"

"Yeah!" Brady said.

"That would be awesome!" I said.

We followed Mr. Putnam through the laboratory, exiting through a set of metal double doors, where we found ourselves in a wide hallway.

"The most exciting thing about my dinosaur exhibits is that you'll find that I replicated the exact habitat for each creature. I created plants and trees from each particular era. I want people to actually feel like they are traveling millions of years back in time, safely strolling among dinosaurs."

We walked until we came to another set of double doors. Mr. Putnam said nothing as he pushed open one door, and we followed him into the interior of the park.

Nothing could prepare me for the unbelievable, incredible sight I was seeing. And, of course, nothing could prepare me for what was about to happen in just a few short minutes.

13

Mr. Putnam was right: it was like stepping back in time, millions and millions of years.

The world within the park looked nothing like Rapid City, South Dakota. High above, the ceiling had been painted to mimic a blue sky with puffy, white clouds. Tall walls rose up three stories to meet the false sky. The inside of the facility was so totally different that it was as if we had left South Dakota and arrived in another country.

There were many plants and trees, although they weren't anything I was familiar with beyond the pages of books. They were exact replicas of plants and trees that had gone extinct long ago, along with the dinosaurs. One tree nearby had leaves the size of garbage can lids!

But by far the most impressive sight were the dinosaurs. From where we stood, I counted eleven, including one that I thought was a replica of a Tyrannosaurus rex. Even though they weren't moving, they looked very, very real. I had been to museums and saw reconstructed dinosaur skeletons, but Mr. Putnam's dinosaurs were like looking at the real thing.

There were numerous large rocks and boulders scattered about, too.

"Even the rocks aren't real," Mr. Putnam explained. "To bring in rocks that size would require enormous trucks, because they would be so heavy, even heavier than the dinosaurs. It could be done, but I found it much easier to make the boulders out of foam. The biggest boulder we have is nearly thirty feet high, but it weighs only a couple hundred pounds."

To demonstrate, he reached down and picked up a rock the size of a volleyball. He walked about ten feet, turned around, and hurled the rock at Brady with all of his might. Brady tried to get out of the way, but he wasn't fast enough. The foam rock hit him, but he barely felt it. It bounced harmlessly to the ground, where he picked it up.

A smile formed on Brady's face as he tossed the foam rock into the air and caught it in his other hand.

"You freaked me out," he said. "It barely weighs anything!" He tossed the foam rock to me, throwing it hard, but I caught it. It couldn't have weighed more than a couple of ounces.

"Come on," Mr. Putnam said. "I'll show you how the dinosaurs work."

We followed Mr. Putnam until we reached a paved path. Although it looked and felt like cement, it was a dusty yellow color, like pollen. This was the path that park visitors would follow as they wound their way through the park to see the various dinosaurs in action.

"Just think," Mr. Putnam said as he proudly spread his arms wide. "In just a little while, hundreds of people will be here, experiencing what life with the dinosaurs was really like."

We walked alongside Mr. Putnam as he pointed out the various names of his dinosaur replicas. Finally, we stopped before one dinosaur that looked suspiciously like a Tyrannosaurus rex. I was just about to ask him if that was what it was, when he spoke.

"I'll bet you think this is a Tyrannosaurus rex, don't you?" he said, smiling and glancing at Brady, and then me.

We bobbed our heads.

"That would be my guess," Brady said.

"Mine, too," I agreed.

Mr. Putnam shook his head. "Close," he said. "In fact, for many years, scientists thought this dinosaur was a close relative of the Tyrannosaurus rex. It's actually a Tarbosaurus, and it existed in the floodplains of Asia around 70 million years ago."

The dinosaur was huge. Monstrous, even. It was over forty feet long.

Mr. Putnam continued. "If this was a real Tarbosaurus," he said, "he would weigh around five tons. This replica weighs about half that. If he was—"

Mr. Putnam was interrupted by a shrill, ringing sound. He dug into his pocket, pulled out his phone, and pressed it to his ear.

"Putnam," he said.

He paused.

His eyes grew wide.

His face looked serious.

He inhaled, then exhaled.

"Okay," he said into the phone. His voice sounded strained and tense. "Don't do anything until I get there. Do you understand?" There was a pause. Then: "I'll be there in just a minute. Don't do anything."

He pocketed his phone.

"I'll be right back," he said. "A little trouble in the command control center. Nothing to worry about. In fact, if you want to continue along the path, by all means, go ahead. I think you'll be fascinated with what you find."

Those little butterflies of nervousness in my stomach returned, fluttering within my rib cage.

A little trouble in the command control center? I thought. *What could that mean?*

One thing we were about to find out: Mr. Putnam had greatly underestimated the size of the problem. What he thought was 'a little trouble' was about to turn into a gigantic nightmare.

14

Mr. Putnam turned on his heels and jogged away.

"He moves pretty fast for an old guy," Brady observed.

"I wonder what the trouble is," I said. "I hope it's nothing serious."

A noise nearby caused us to turn.

"Hey," Brady said. "Check that out. The Tarbosaurus is moving."

As we watched, the dinosaur replica slowly

moved his front legs, which were much smaller than his longer, thicker hind legs.

It blinked. Then, it sniffed the air.

We watched, amazed and mystified.

"That's incredible," Brady whispered. *"That thing really looks like it's alive!"*

All around us, dinosaurs began to move. Every single one of them looked like they were alive. I guess I had expected their movements to be a bit jerky and stiff, but Mr. Putnam was right: their movements were deliberate and very lifelike. It was one of the most amazing experiences I'd ever had. I never dreamed I would actually be able to see dinosaurs in their actual environment. Sure, they weren't real . . . but it was impossible to tell the difference.

The Tarbosaurus began walking, and his feet shook the earth. I knew that the thing was only a battery-powered, computer-programmed robot, but I couldn't help but think that the creature was looking at us. Brady noticed it, too.

"It looks like his eyes are focused on us," he

said.

"Mr. Putnam sure thought of everything," I replied. "That thing even blinks its eyes."

But as the giant dinosaur continued to move closer, I began to get nervous. I became more nervous when his sinister, dark eyes remained on us, never looking away.

Somewhere in the park, an alarm rang out. It was just like the one we'd heard in the command control center: a shrill, high-pitched screech. It echoed through the park, and several dinosaurs turned, distracted by the noise.

But they're not real, I thought. *Why would an alarm disturb them?*

The noise drew the attention of the Tarbosaurus, but not for long. In one swift movement, he returned his attention to us and opened his jaws, displaying enormous, curved, sharp teeth. He sniffed the air again and let out a snarl. Then, with no warning whatsoever, he began charging toward us!

I screamed and ran off to the left. There was no time to think about anything else except getting away from the creature. Regardless of whether or not it was a robot, that thing was coming after us!

I ran to one of the enormous boulders. From there, I had no idea what I would do, but I was safe for the time being. The Tarbosaurus hadn't come after me . . . but he was giving Brady some real trouble.

Brady had fled in the opposite direction, but the only place he could hide was behind a clump of fake trees. The trunks were quite large, nearly twice his size, but I doubted they would keep the Tarbosaurus from getting at him. Right now, the dinosaur was in front of the trees with his enormous snout near the trunks. Brady was on the other side of the trunks, using them as a barricade between him and the dinosaur. For the moment, it was working. But I knew that if the Tarbosaurus wanted to get him, all it had to do was knock down the trees. After all: they weren't even real trees. The powerful dinosaur could easily crush them, just as easily as he could crush Brady.

How can this be? I thought. *The dinosaurs aren't even real. How is it that these things can have minds of their own?*

I looked around for any sign of Mr. Putnam or anyone that might come to help us. Surely, other people must know that we were in the park. Somebody must be coming to get us out of here.

I saw no one. The only things I saw were

dinosaurs moving about the park, on their own. What once had been fascinating was now horrifying.

These things really are alive, I thought. *I know it's impossible. They don't have flesh and blood and brains like real dinosaurs, but somehow, these creatures have come alive. It really does seem like they have minds of their own.*

I wasn't in immediate danger, but I had to think. I needed to find a way to help Brady. He was still playing peek-a-boo with the enormous Tarbosaurus, and if he didn't get away soon, I knew the end result wasn't going to be good.

At the same time, I had to worry about the other dinosaurs. I was mostly hidden behind the large boulder, and I was sure most of the dinosaurs couldn't see me. Somehow, I needed to get Brady's attention so he could, at the very least, know where I was and know that I was safe.

During this time, the alarm had continued to screech. It suddenly stopped, and the only sounds we could hear were the dinosaurs themselves.

Some of them were grunting and growling. Far off, a dinosaur let out a loud, vicious roar.

The roar drew the attention of the Tarbosaurus. He backed away from the tree and turned his head, cocking it curiously to the side.

"Brady!" I shouted. I tried to be loud enough for him to hear me, but not loud enough to attract attention. I also stepped out a little bit from behind the boulder and waved my arm so that Brady could see where I was.

It worked. Brady saw me. He snapped his head around to make sure there were no other dinosaurs near him. Then, he took another glance at the Tarbosaurus, which was still looking the other way, distracted by the distant roar.

Instantly, Brady sprang from his hiding place and began running toward me.

The Tarbosaurus turned his head.

Brady continued running.

And if a robot dinosaur could look angry, the Tarbosaurus appeared to be *enraged*. He snorted like a bull, snarled like a tiger, opened his mouth, and gave chase. His feet pounded the ground, and I could feel the earth shaking beneath my feet with every step.

Brady wasn't going to have a chance.

16

Each day at school, we learn a new word. Sometimes, I forget them, but once in a while one sticks with me.

One of those words that I remembered was *surreal*. It means 'resembling a dream.'

That word popped into my head as I watched the forty-foot dinosaur chasing my friend. Brady looked like a little toy compared to the monstrous reptile that was hot on his tail.

This is surreal, I thought, remembering the word. *This is like something out of a dream. Or a nightmare.*

Brady was running as fast as his legs would carry him. Every few seconds, he would glance over his shoulder to get a glimpse of the dinosaur.

I had never been so freaked out, so horrified in my entire life. Thoughts spun in my head like a swarm of crazed hornets.

Even if Brady reached the boulder where I was, then what? What would the Tarbosaurus do then?

And where was Mr. Putnam? How come there were no other people around? Was help on the way, or were we on our own?

For the time being, I had to figure that we were on our own. I had to plan what to do in case no one came to help us.

I looked behind the boulder. At the bottom of it, there was a small space between the ground and the rock. Which, of course, wasn't really rock, but that didn't matter. What mattered was that the space was big enough for Brady and me to crawl into, but not big enough for the dinosaur to get at us. Of course, if the Tarbosaurus was *really* serious, he could just push the giant boulder out of the way. Mr. Putnam said it weighed only a couple of hundred pounds, and I was certain that the mechanical dinosaur wouldn't have any trouble pushing the boulder and moving it around to get at us. Then, it would be all over for us.

However, we were faced with no other choice.

I dropped to my knees, fell to the ground, and crawled into the space. I could only hope that Brady was fast enough.

"Hurry!" I screamed. *"That thing is right behind you!"*

With a surprising burst of speed, Brady managed to put some distance between himself and the raging Tarbosaurus. When he was only a few feet from the boulder, he leapt and dove, flying through the air with his arms in front of him like Superman. He hit the ground with a thud, rolled, and quickly scrambled to the wedge-like space beneath the rock.

"You made it!" I said.

Brady was so out of breath and gasping for air that he couldn't reply.

But we weren't out of trouble yet.

Without question, the Tarbosaurus knew where we were hiding. In fact, you couldn't even really call it 'hiding.' The dinosaur could easily see us. He bent down, stretched his neck, and pushed his head forward. His nose touched the boulder, and he opened his mouth. His tongue lashed out, and I wondered what material Mr. Putnam had used to create it. It looked like the real thing: soft and fleshy and pink. It even appeared wet, as if it was covered with a sheen of slobbery saliva.

Maybe Mr. Putnam went a little bit too far, I thought.

Brady squeezed farther into the wedge, closer to me, away from the dinosaur's mouth and his razor-sharp teeth. Still, the Tarbosaurus tried to get at us. Apparently, the creature didn't realize that the boulder wasn't really made of rock, because the beast made no attempt to move it.

After a few seconds, when he realized he couldn't reach us, he backed away. After another moment, he stormed off in another direction.

Brady was still gasping for breath, but he managed to speak.

"Those things are alive!" he said. "Robots don't act like that! That thing came after me! I was almost a dinosaur appetizer!"

"I don't know what's going on," I said, "but Mr. Putnam knows we're here. He won't leave us in danger. Either he'll be back soon, or he's already sent help. We'll be safe under this rock. All we have to do is wait."

We waited.

Help never arrived.

Waiting for help seemed to go on and on, and the longer we waited, the more hopeless our situation seemed. It felt like the seconds turned into hours, the hours turned into days.

And while I knew we were in Rapid City,

South Dakota, it felt like we really had traveled back in time, millions of years, to the era when brutal reptiles ruled the land.

I also knew this: if we were going to survive, it was going to be up to us.

17

After about twenty minutes, I realized that Mr. Putnam's 'little trouble' had turned into a major disaster. I didn't know what was wrong or why it happened, and I didn't know why help had not arrived, but I knew that something had gone seriously wrong.

"They must know that things have gone crazy," Brady said. "They must know that all of the dinosaurs are completely out of control."

We watched the many dinosaurs as they wandered about the park. All the while, we remained on the lookout for a vehicle or anything that might indicate help had arrived. We saw nothing.

"I don't understand why they don't shut them off," I said. "Mr. Putnam said all the dinosaurs are controlled by remote computers. Why don't they just shut them off?"

"Maybe something has overridden the systems," Brady replied. "The good news is that, sooner or later, their batteries will run down. When that happens, they'll stop moving. All we have to do is be patient and wait. As long as we're tucked under this rock, we're safe."

"Hey," I said as I reached into my sweatshirt. It was difficult, because I was laying on my side, packed against the rock and the ground. Plus, Brady was in front of me, so I didn't have much room to move.

"What?" Brady asked.

"I have my digital camera. I'm going to take

some pictures."

I managed to pull my camera from my pocket. I turned it on and gave it to Brady, as he was in a better position to take some pictures.

"Get a couple of shots of some of the dinosaurs," I said. "It also takes videos, so make a little movie. When we get out of here, it'll be great to show everyone."

Brady took my camera. Every time he took a picture, there was a little musical 'ding' that sounded.

"There's a cool-looking dinosaur over there," Brady said. "I'll take a video of him."

He pointed the camera at a smaller dinosaur that was about fifty feet away from us. For some reason, the dinosaur looked familiar. I was certain that I must have read about it in a book. It was a bit taller than a human, but it was about twenty feet long: about half the size of the Tarbosaurus. It walked on its hind legs and looked quite vicious. As it got closer, I could see that its front claws appeared to be wing-like, and they even had feathers. Additionally, there was a shock of prickly, thick hair stretching down the creature's back. It was almost as if the dinosaur was in a stage of mid-evolution, part land animal and part bird.

While Brady shot the video, I watched the dinosaur.

The dinosaur watched us.

Cautiously, he started moving in our direction. The dinosaur moved slowly, taking careful, stealthy steps.

Fear knotted in my gut.

I've seen that dinosaur before, I thought. *I've seen pictures of it. Where?*

The dinosaur continued coming toward us. His movements were slow, deliberate, and carefully thought out.

The fear in my gut twisted my intestines in a tight knot. That fear turned into complete horror when I realized that I knew the name of the dinosaur. I recognized him.

Achillobator. The Achilles Warrior. One of the most barbaric hunters of the late Cretaceous era, from about 90 million years ago. Although the Achillobator is a dinosaur not many people know about, it was one that I had picked to do a report on in school. The Achillobator was given that name because scientists and paleontologists widely agreed that, because of the position of its hips, it must've had enormous Achilles tendons, which is the tissue that connects the heel to the lower leg muscles.

But I also knew that the Achillobator was an absolutely ruthless killer. He was about half the size of the Tarbosaurus and quite a bit smaller than a Tyrannosaurus rex . . . which meant that the Achillobator would have no trouble crouching down and tearing us from our hiding place.

We were out of time. We couldn't wait any longer.

It was time to make a run for it.

18

"Brady," I said quietly, "give me the camera, and move real slow. We have to get out of here."

"Are you nuts, Autumn?" he replied. "We're in the only safe place around."

"Not for long," I said. "That thing is an Achillobator, and he won't have any trouble getting at us."

"I've never heard of them," Brady said.

"Most people haven't," I replied. "But I did a

report on them for school. They're one of the most vicious, meat-eating dinosaurs that ever lived. They have teeth that are over four inches long, and they're shaped like steak knives. If Mr. Putnam programmed all of his dinosaurs to act like the real thing, we're going to be in a lot of trouble."

"I've got news for you," Brady said. "We already *are* in a lot of trouble."

Brady handed the camera back to me, and for whatever reason, the Achillobator stopped. The robot-dinosaur looked at us curiously, as if trying to decide if we were food.

I looked around the park as best I could from my hiding place. From where I lay, I couldn't really see a lot, but I was looking for someplace to go where we wouldn't encounter any dinosaurs. Someplace that we could hide, out of sight, until help finally arrived.

But mechanical dinosaurs were everywhere. They were wandering all over the place. No matter where we went, no matter where we ran, we would encounter dinosaurs of all species, sizes, and shapes. Some were plant eaters, and some were meat eaters. Some of them might leave us alone, but others, like the Tarbosaurus, might threaten us.

Like the Achillobator.

Right now, he wasn't a threat. We watched him watching us, and I tried to get into his mind. I tried to think what he was thinking.

Then, I realized once again: *he doesn't have a mind. He's a battery-powered robot, programmed by a computer.*

Still, that wasn't much comfort. The Tarbosaurus had attacked us, and there is no doubt in my mind that if he'd gotten a hold of one of us, we would've been torn to shreds. Obviously, Mr. Putnam had some work to do before he opened his park to the public. He couldn't open up his place to people if his dinosaurs were going to have an all-you-can-eat human smorgasbord.

"What's that thing doing?" Brady asked.

I shook my head. "I don't know," I replied. "I just hope he decides we're not worth his effort. Do you see his claws? He looks kind of goofy with his front arms that look like wings, but his claws are razor-sharp. They're meant for one thing, and one thing only."

"Don't tell me," Brady said, shaking his head. "I don't want to know."

We were still hunkered down in our tight, cramped little hiding space. The Achillobator took another step toward us.

Then another.

And another.

With every step he took, my heart beat faster.

"Get ready to run," I whispered.

"Where?" Brady whispered back. *"There are dinosaurs everywhere."*

"I don't know," I said quietly. *"But I think we're going to have to make a run for it."*

"Maybe if we just move slowly, none of them will bother us," Brady suggested.

We wouldn't get a chance to find out.

The Achillobator lowered his head. He

leaned forward and raised his right leg into the air. When he plunged it back to the earth, he was in a full-bore run toward us.

"Get up!" I shrieked. *"Run!"*

We scrambled to our feet and took flight, not knowing where we would go, not knowing if we would even survive.

19

In seconds, we were running as fast as our legs could take us. Now that we were out in the open, I searched for a safe haven, someplace where the dinosaurs couldn't get us, but I found nothing.

In the distance, I could see the tall wall of the park, stretching up to meet the sky-painted ceiling high above.

"That way!" I shouted. "We need to find an emergency exit!"

"We'll never make it that far!" Brady shouted.

"It's better than staying here and being human ham sandwiches for that dinosaur!" I shouted as we ran.

I shot a glance over my shoulder, and I realized there was no way we would outrun the Achillobator. While Brady and I were running as fast as we could, the Achillobator's movements seemed almost effortless. It was as if he was toying with us, allowing us to stay just ahead of him, waiting until we were too tired to continue running.

Maybe that's what he's going to do, I thought. *Maybe he's going to wait until we're exhausted, when we have no fight left within us. Then, we'd be easy prey.*

But then, help arrived in a very unexpected fashion. It wasn't Mr. Putnam that saved us, and it wasn't a crew of rescuers.

It was another dinosaur.

From out of nowhere, another dinosaur

charged the Achillobator, who was forced to abandon his pursuit of us and defend himself from the attacking reptile.

It was the break we needed. Although there were many other dinosaurs in the park, most of them paid no attention to us as we threaded around trees and enormous boulders.

"Keep looking for a place to hide!" I shouted.

"I don't see anything!" Brady replied.

We continued running, heading for the wall. I was certain that if we could only make it there, we'd find a door, an emergency exit, or someplace we could go to be safe. I was also certain that we were being watched in the command control center. People must be aware of what was happening and what we were up against. They must be assembling a rescue team at that very moment.

It seemed to take forever, but we finally reached the tall brick wall. It was the first time I'd seen it up close, and it was fascinating. The entire wall, from the bottom to the top, was a mural painting depicting the current surroundings. The painting contained rocks, boulders, trees, and shrubs, just like the ones contained in the park. There were also paintings of dinosaurs. The effect was an optical illusion of sorts, as it appeared to make the wall vanish. It looked as if the landscape just continued on and on into the distance.

But if there were any doors, the painting made them difficult to see. I looked for familiar red *Emergency Exit* signs, but there were none.

"Let's keep going along the wall," I said.

We were still running, but both of us were tiring quickly.

"I can't keep going much longer," Brady said. "I'm getting tired."

"I am, too," I said. "But we have to keep going. There has to be a door somewhere. Even if it's just a restroom, that would give us a place to hide."

And, like magic, we suddenly came across a sign on the wall. In big, bold letters, it read:

RESTROOMS

Beneath that sign were two arrows, pointing to two separate doors, one for men, and one for women. The doors were nearly impossible to see because they were painted with the park scene that covered the entire wall.

But there were two more signs, one on each door, that read:

CLOSED FOR CONSTRUCTION

"There!" I shouted. *"Go!"*

Once again, luck was with us when we reached one of the doors. I was worried that it would be locked because of the construction going on, but that wasn't the case. I pushed the door, and it swayed open. We wasted no time slipping inside and closing the door behind us. I found the light switch and flipped it up. There was a deadbolt on the door, and I quickly slid it to its locked position.

Brady leaned against the wall and slid to the floor. I stood in the middle of the room, hands on my hips, catching my breath.

"We made it," he said, his lungs heaving.

I was breathing heavily, too. It felt like my lungs were on fire.

But we were alive. We had made it to the safety of the restroom.

The only thing we didn't realize at the time was that the door was our only way out, and if a dinosaur blocked our exit, or worse—if one of them came through the door—there would be no place for us to go.

We would be cornered.

No, that was something we didn't realize . . . until it was far too late.

20

I joined Brady on the floor, leaning against the opposite wall so we were facing one another. My skin was glossed with a film of sweat, and wearing my sweatshirt made me even warmer. I pulled it up over my head and put it on the floor next to me.

Brady looked at my shirt. He laughed.

"You know," he said with a smile, "that's actually quite funny."

I looked down at my shirt. On the front of it was a very vicious looking Tyrannosaurus rex. Beneath it was a caption that read: *I ♥ dinosaurs*. Mom and Dad had given it to me earlier in the year as a birthday gift.

I had to smile. Even after everything we had been through, my shirt made me laugh.

"We're safe now," I said. "Now, all we have to do is wait. There's no doubt someone will be coming soon."

I looked around the restroom. The floor, walls, and ceiling were finished, but there was still some work to be done. The bathroom stall was in the process of being painted, and there were no cupboards around the sink. A white porcelain sink hung from the wall, and two pipes were connected to the bottom of it: hot and cold water. The pipes vanished into the floor.

Beyond the bathroom door, we could hear the occasional snarl and roar of the dinosaurs in the park. Once in a while, the floor and walls shook.

Then, we heard a scratching at the door. It sounded like fingernails on a blackboard, and it made my skin crawl. We knew it was a dinosaur, but not being able to see outside, we had no idea what kind or how big it was.

I raised a finger to my lips, indicating to Brady to remain quiet. He nodded.

The scratch came again. This time, it sounded like several sharp claws dragging along the door.

"Do you think he knows we're in here?" Brady whispered.

I shook my head. *"How could he?"* I whispered back. *"They're just robots. They can't smell."*

"Maybe so," Brady replied quietly, *"but they can certainly see pretty good."*

Brady had a good point. If they truly were mechanical robots, how could they see us? Perhaps their eyes were like cameras containing motion detectors. Maybe that's how they saw us. It was something I would ask Mr. Putnam after we were rescued.

The scratch came once again, louder this time. As quietly as we could, Brady and I moved farther away from the door until we were backed up against the bathroom stall.

"You know," Brady whispered, *"if one of those dinosaurs breaks down the door, we have nowhere to go."*

Brady's revelation took hold, and once again, my stomach knotted with fear. I looked around the bathroom. There were no windows, only a small vent in the ceiling that wasn't big enough for us to fit through.

Brady was right: if a dinosaur decided to break down the door to get to us, it would block our only way out. We were totally helpless, defenseless.

But the realization came too late. Even if we decided to leave, to try to find a better hiding place, that idea was out of the question.

Suddenly, the restroom door exploded inward, breaking into two pieces as it crashed violently to the floor. Brady and I, backed against the bathroom stall, could only stare at the horrific beast that filled the doorway. With its piercing eyes, menacing teeth, and claws made for ripping and tearing flesh, there was no mistaking what we were looking at.

An Allosaurus.

21

If the creature that was staring back at us was a dinosaur, he was also a thief, for he had stolen our breaths.

I spoke to Brady as softly as I could, pausing briefly after each word. *"Don't. Move. An. Inch."*

The face of the Allosaurus staring back at us looked very similar to the ones I'd seen in books and movies. However, seeing one up close, in real life, regardless of whether or not it was a robot, was completely different. Nothing I'd ever seen could compare to what this dinosaur looked like and the terror it inspired.

Most of his head and snout filled the doorway, so we couldn't see his body. But I knew from the books that I read that a typical Allosaurus grew up to forty feet long and could weigh three tons or more.

His eyes were as black as coal, the size of softballs, and they glared at us with a hatred that was inhuman. Staring into those eyes, it was hard to believe that the creature was a mere robot, incapable of thoughts, feelings, and emotions.

But maybe Mr. Putnam had built them that way. Maybe he wanted them to look like they were mean and hateful, just to make them more scary.

If so, it worked.

The Allosaurus drew back his head and reached toward us with one of his upper legs. The claw entered the doorway, reaching in, farther, farther still . . . .

Brady and I were backed against the stall. I

tried to open the door to it, but it was either locked or sealed shut.

Enormous claws twisted and turned a few inches from us; the Allosaurus's legs weren't quite long enough to reach us.

Slowly, the Allosaurus withdrew his leg, but he was far from giving up. He began tearing at the doorway with his claw, ripping the molding apart, tearing chunks of wood and metal away.

"He's tearing a bigger doorway!" Brady shrieked. *"He's making the doorway bigger, so he can get at us!"*

I looked around the restroom with a horrified resignation. Unless someone came to our rescue within the next few seconds—and that didn't seem very likely—we were going to be human hot wings for a ravenous reptile.

But then I saw the sink and the two pipes connected to it.

Hot and cold water.

Suddenly, I remembered something that happened at our house, and I had an idea. It was a long shot, and it probably wouldn't work. But I had to try. I had to make one last ditch effort to save our lives.

But my idea posed two questions: would it work, and, if so, could I do it fast enough?

I was about to find out.

22

This is what I remembered that gave me my idea:

Last year, the cold water pipe attached to our kitchen sink broke beneath the cupboard. When a pipe breaks, water doesn't just leak out—it sprays wildly, because of constant pressure. If it isn't capped, it will continue to spray and spray and spray.

Fortunately, my dad knew what to do, and he went down into our basement and shut off the water valve, which stopped the water from spraying out and flooding the kitchen. But we still had a mess to clean up.

Remembering that gave me an idea.

If I can break one of those pipes, I thought, *water will spray out. That Allosaurus is made of electrical parts. If those parts get wet, maybe he'll stop working.*

I didn't tell Brady my plan; there was no time. I simply sprang to the sink, fell to my knees, and grasped one of the pipes.

"What are you doing?!?!" Brady shouted.

"I'm going to break this pipe!" I shouted back. "Help me!"

"What are you doing that for?" Brady asked.

"You'll see!" I said. "Just help me!"

Meanwhile, the Allosaurus was relentless, continuously ripping and tearing at the doorway. I knew it wouldn't be very long before he tore a hole wide enough to fit his head through.

I pulled and pulled with all my might. I tried to twist the pipe, but that didn't work, either.

Brady rushed to my side and helped. Even with the both of us tugging on it, we couldn't get it to break. Finally, I stood.

"Get back!" I shouted.

Brady stepped away from the sink and turned to watch the giant Allosaurus continue to gnaw at the doorway.

I drew back my right leg and kicked the pipe as hard as I could.

There was a snap and a sudden hiss of spewing water as the pipe broke off just beneath the sink. I grabbed it and bent it like a garden hose, aiming the stream of water at the door and the attacking Allosaurus. I found I could easily guide the spray at the reptile's face. Most important, I tried to get the water into his mouth and nose whenever I could, which was often, because he was now using his powerful jaws to tear away the rest of the doorway.

"You can't stop that thing with water!" Brady screeched. "Have you gone completely bonkers?"

"You're forgetting that it's not really a dinosaur," I shouted. "It's a piece of electronics. If I can soak his circuitry, he might stop working!"

"I don't see how—"

Brady was interrupted by a popping sound and a loud sizzle. Smoke began to pour from the nostrils and mouth of the Allosaurus. His head began to shake back and forth.

"Holy smokes!" Brady shouted. "It's working! It's really working!"

"I told you!" I said. "Water and electricity don't mix."

The Allosaurus was definitely having trouble. He was having problems functioning, and his head started banging against the doorway. He was no longer tearing at it, and he didn't seem to have control over his movements.

Finally, he backed away from the door, and we could see the full size of his body. He was enormous, about the same size as the Tarbosaurus, although he looked quite different.

His entire body shook violently. Then, as if

a plug had been pulled or a switch had been thrown, he stopped moving altogether. Yet, when he did, he was off balance.

"He's going to tip over!" Brady said.

We watched as the enormous Allosaurus leaned sideways, farther, farther still, until his body slammed into the ground with a spectacular, thundering crash. The building around us trembled and shook.

Then, an odd stillness came over us. Outside, in the park, we could still see other dinosaurs wandering about. But the Allosaurus in front of us lay on its side, with sparks and smoke coming from its mouth and nostrils.

"That was brilliant, Autumn," Brady said. "I thought we were done for."

I still had hold of the pipe in my right hand, and a ten-foot spray of water still continued to spew from it. My jeans and shirt had gotten a little wet, but I didn't care. That was the least of my concerns. If I got wet and the place got flooded a little bit, so what? We were alive, and that's what was important.

Brady spoke. "When is this going to be over?" he asked. "When is this nightmare going to end?"

"Soon, I hope," I said. "Soon."

23

We were sure that help would arrive sooner or later. The problem was that it might not arrive in time. While we remained in the restroom, we were at the mercy of any dinosaur that wanted to come after us. Yes, the water continued to spray, but there was no guarantee that it would work again.

For instance, if one of the smaller dinosaurs decided to attack us, it could easily charge into the restroom and tear us apart before I had a chance to spray it with water.

So, we had to come up with another plan.

Brady and I stood in the doorway, looking into the park. We watched dinosaurs roaming beneath tropical trees. For the most part, they left one another alone. But every so often, a fight would break out.

"I wonder if Mr. Putnam programmed them that way," Brady said.

"What way?" I asked.

"To fight like that," he replied. "I mean, I'm sure that dinosaurs got into fights all the time. But the way these dinosaurs are fighting, they don't seem to be paying any attention to what's going on around them. If there are people wandering around and a dinosaur fight breaks out, somebody might get hurt."

"Another question for Mr. Putnam," I said, "when we get out of here."

"Any brilliant ideas?" Brady asked.

"As a matter of fact," I answered, "yes. I say we leave the restroom and follow the wall. From where we are right now, we can't see any doors. But there has to be some emergency exit, or something. In fact, there has to be a big door somewhere. A door big enough for trucks to come in and out for loading and unloading."

"Not to mention a door big enough for that dinosaur we saw this morning," Brady said. "The one that Mr. Putnam said was being tested."

I remembered seeing the dinosaur behind the park when we first arrived and how horrified we had been when we thought it ate a man. I remembered how silly I felt when we found out that it wasn't really a man, after all.

"So, let's go," I said. "Let's move slowly, stay against the wall, and keep going until we find a door."

"Or until one of those things eats us," Brady said.

Slowly, we left the restroom and began creeping along the wall. Soon, we could no longer hear the water spewing from the pipe. The only sounds we heard came from the dinosaurs. The bigger ones caused the ground to tremble when they walked, and we constantly heard distant roaring and snarling.

But we stayed against the wall and went slowly, and none of the mechanical reptiles seemed to notice us.

It was Brady who spotted the big door first. He had been right: there was a huge door at the back of the park. It stretched all the way to the top of the wall, making it three stories tall. It was a double door that opened in the center; whether it opened outward or inward was anybody's guess.

We stopped when we reached it. Like the restroom doors, it, too, was painted with the park scene. From a distance, you wouldn't even know it was a door.

"All we have to do is find a way to open it," I said. "Look around for a button of some sort."

"If it's operated by remote control, like the dinosaurs," Brady said, "we're going to be out of luck."

While we searched, we kept a careful eye on

the dinosaurs. Some of them roamed quite close to us. When they did, we stopped moving, pressing ourselves against the wall. Thankfully, we didn't have any more trouble.

"I think I found it!" Brady shouted suddenly. "It's hard to see because it's painted."

I walked to where Brady stood in front of the wall. There were three quarter-sized buttons in a vertical row. Because they were painted to match the wall, the buttons were nearly invisible.

I pressed the bottom one. Nothing happened. I pressed the middle one.

Nothing.

Then, I pressed the top button.

Bingo!

The doors began to move, swinging open outward. The process was slow, but within a few seconds, we were able to see outside. Not far away, we could see houses and some of the taller buildings of Rapid City.

"We made it!" Brady said. "We made it out!"

"Hang on," I said. "We need to make sure

the doors close behind us. We can't have—"

A terrifying roar stopped me in mid-sentence. Had it not been so close, I wouldn't have been concerned. But the dinosaur that had made the sound was close, and he sounded big.

Brady and I turned.

About a hundred feet away was a dinosaur that was unmistakable. A dinosaur anyone would recognize. A dinosaur that was a natural born killer.

A Tyrannosaurus rex.

24

We stood motionless, watching the enormous dinosaur. I was surprised we hadn't heard him approach, but when the Tyrannosaurus moved, I suddenly knew why. His steps were slow and cautious, despite his gigantic size.

He was stalking us.

"This is getting really, really old," Brady said.

Behind us, the giant double doors were now

completely open. I simply wanted to run, but we couldn't leave without closing the doors behind us. What would happen if the dinosaurs got out?

"Okay," I said quickly and quietly. "Here's what we're going to do. I'm going to press the button to close the doors. We should have enough time to get out before they close completely. That way we'll be safely outside, and the dinosaurs won't be able to get out."

"Sounds good to me," Brady said. "Let's get moving. That Tyrannosaurus rex is getting closer and closer."

"Go!" I said.

Brady ran outside, while I pressed the bottom button. It seemed only logical that button would be the one to close the door; luckily, I had been right. As soon as I pressed it, the huge double doors began to close.

"Hurry, Autumn!" Brady shouted. "The T. rex is moving faster!"

He didn't have to tell me that, because I could hear the thunder of the monster dinosaur's feet pounding the ground, and I knew it wouldn't be very long before he reached the wall. By then, the doors would be closed, and Brady and I would be safely outside.

I sprinted through the doorway with plenty of time to spare. Now, it was a nail-biting waiting game to see if the doors would close in time.

But we weren't going to spend that precious time standing around. No way. We were going to run as fast as we could and get as far away as possible. I didn't know who to tell first: the police or Mr. Putnam. After all, Mr. Putnam needed to know that we were safe. He needed to know we made it out of the park alive.

"To the front of the park!" I said. "Maybe the box office is open, and we can get in that way."

"I don't think they'll be opening the park just yet," Brady said as we ran. "They can't let people inside the park while the dinosaurs are still going crazy."

Behind us we heard a heavy thunk. I managed a quick glance over my shoulder and saw that the double doors had closed.

"That was too close," I said. "That Tyrannosaurus rex wanted us bad."

I spoke too soon.

Suddenly, we heard an enormous crash. The sound came from behind us, and we both stopped and turned.

My heart felt like it was in my throat. That familiar twisted knot of fear that I'd felt earlier came back once again, only this time it was as if someone was clamping a vice around my stomach.

The double doors had been blown open by the Tyrannosaurus rex, and now the dinosaur was standing outside of the park, inspecting his new surroundings.

That was bad, but it was about to get worse.

While we watched, the Tyrannosaurus rex began walking. Other dinosaurs were following him. First there was one, then two. Then three and four. More followed. Still more.

"This just gets worse and worse," Brady breathed.

I was scared, and I felt horrible. Oh, I was thankful we made it out alive, don't get me wrong. But in doing so, we'd allowed vicious dinosaurs to escape the park.

And for my hometown of Rapid City, South Dakota, the carnage was about to begin.

25

"We've got to warn everyone!" Brady shouted.

"Let's keep going to the front of the building," I said. "There has to be somebody there who can help us. We need to call the police."

"And the Army," Brady said as we turned and began to run again. "And the Navy, Air Force, and Marines. It's going to take all of them to stop those things."

Finally, we made it to the front of the

building. By then, the parking lot was filling up. When we first arrived, there were only a few cars. Now, there were a couple hundred. There was a huge line that had formed in front of the box office. Everyone was waiting to buy tickets.

"We have to warn everyone," Brady said.

I shook my head. "How?" I asked. "If we start telling people the dinosaurs are loose, they're just going to panic. Or they won't believe us, and they'll think we're crazy."

"They're not going to think we're crazy when dinosaurs begin to stomp all over their cars," Brady said. "I'm telling you: we have to warn them."

"Maybe so," I said, "but we've got to think. We've got to be smart about this. Maybe we should find Mr. Putnam first. He would know what to do."

"He's the guy who said that there was 'a little trouble,'" Brady snapped. "Come on, Autumn. This isn't just a *little* trouble. This is a *catastrophe*. It's a disaster. Mr. Putnam might be a smart inventor, but I think he's too smart for his own good. He has no idea what he has created. And if he does, he sure doesn't know how to control his creations."

"You might be right," I agreed, "but it's no reason to cause people to panic. When people panic, they do stupid things. More people could get hurt by panicking than from the dinosaurs."

"Do you think he's going to get into trouble for this?" Brady asked.

"Who?" I replied.

"Mr. Putnam," Brady said. "He's the one who created those robotic dinosaurs. It's his fault."

I thought about this, and I felt bad for Mr. Putnam. Yes, we could have been killed. But Mr. Putnam genuinely wanted to do a good thing. He wanted to live his dream, and share it with others. I'm certain that if he knew lives would be put in danger, he never would've proceeded.

"If he gets into trouble," I said, "I will stand by him. He might have made some mistakes, but he didn't mean to. He's a smart man and a nice guy. And besides: we haven't been hurt. We managed to get out safely. There really has been no harm done."

"Yet," Brady said. "Those dinosaurs have gotten out of the park. Nobody seems to have control over them. If they're not stopped, things are going to get pretty ugly really quick."

I tried not to think about that. I tried not to think about what would happen if the Tyrannosaurus rex decided to take a leisurely stroll through downtown Rapid City. There's no doubt he would wind up crushing cars and knocking over buildings.

And that's what I was thinking about when someone in the parking lot screamed.

26

Brady and I had just rounded the front of the building and were jogging toward the box office. The line of people extended from the front doors and far into the parking lot. Up until then, everything had been calm. People were waiting patiently, laughing and talking in the line.

When we heard someone scream, we stopped and turned.

It was a woman. She was pointing into the

distance. We turned, and everyone else in the line looked at what she was pointing at. In the field between the park and a subdivision of houses was the Tyrannosaurus rex. Several other dinosaurs were in its wake, walking purposefully toward the city, looking around curiously.

But they're not real, I told myself. *They're just robots. Why are they acting like that? Why are they acting like real, live creatures?*

"So," Brady began, "who's going to get in trouble?"

"What do you mean?" I replied.

"I mean just that: who's going to get into trouble? Mr. Putnam, or us?"

I never took my eyes off the dinosaurs during our discussion.

"What are you talking about?" I asked. "How can we get into trouble?"

"We were the ones who opened the door," Brady replied. "If it wasn't for us, those dinosaurs wouldn't be loose."

"But they haven't done anything," I replied.

"*Yet,*" Brady said. "They haven't done anything, *yet.* But look where they're headed. There must be twenty dinosaurs out there, and they're all headed toward the downtown area."

I was bewildered. Brady did have a point. When it came right down to it, we were responsible for letting the dinosaurs out. We would be responsible for what happened now. But what happened next was so crazy, so unbelievable, my mind failed to grasp it.

The people that had been waiting in line began to rush toward the dinosaurs. Most had cameras, and they headed straight for the reptiles, intent on getting the best possible pictures. They thought the dinosaurs were harmless, and they probably figured that it was all part of the show, part of the park.

Those poor people were about to find out they were wrong.

Dead wrong.

27

We rushed toward the crowd of people who were moving in the direction of the dinosaurs. Everyone was smiling and laughing, thinking that the wandering dinosaurs were just part of the entertainment. They had no idea how dangerous they really were.

Brady and I waived our arms and shook our heads.

"No!" I shouted. "Stop! The dinosaurs are

dangerous!"

"Don't get close to them!" Brady said. "The dinosaurs will attack you!"

No one paid any attention to us. They continued running across the parking lot until it ended at the field. Then, they waded through the tall grass and continued toward the dinosaurs.

The Tyrannosaurus rex stopped moving when he heard the commotion.

All of the other dinosaurs stopped moving, too.

They turned and looked at the horde of people coming toward them.

A couple of people stopped and clicked pictures. Others continued to run toward the dinosaurs, intent on getting close-up shots of the reptiles.

"This is going to be horrible," I said. "Those people don't know how dangerous the dinosaurs are."

"Don't they know that something is wrong?" Brady asked.

I shook my head. "No," I said. "Probably not. They're thinking that it must be one of the park's attractions. They have no idea that the dinosaurs are malfunctioning."

By now, the crowd was approaching the herd of dinosaurs. Most people had cameras, and they were clicking picture after picture.

The dinosaurs had stopped moving. They were watching the people curiously, as if they were seeing strange and different animals. Men and women chatted and laughed, amazed at the gigantic creatures.

From the crowd, a single man broke away. He was carrying a large camera with a long, black lens. It was a professional camera, much different from the small pocket digital cameras that most people were carrying. He held the camera to his eye with one hand and supported the lens with the other as he approached one of the dinosaurs.

"We've got to do something," Brady said.

I shook my head. "We're too far away," I said. "We'll never get there in time. Besides: we tried to warn everyone. We already tried to stop them. Nothing we say will change their minds, until they learn for themselves."

The man with the big camera was only a few feet away from one of the dinosaurs. I didn't recognize the reptile, but I knew one thing: he sure looked vicious. He was easily three times the size of the man with the camera.

And the beast didn't look very pleased.

While this was going on, the other dinosaurs were still staring curiously at the crowd of people, who continued to chat among themselves and take pictures. Even the giant Tyrannosaurus rex seemed puzzled. He faced the crowd with an expression of curiosity and wonder, cocking his head sideways the way a dog does when it hears a high-pitched sound.

The man with the large camera circled the dinosaur he'd been photographing. He was fearless, walking right up to the creature, just a few feet away, and taking close-up shots of the reptile's head and face.

"I'm getting a really, really bad feeling about this," Brady said.

I said nothing. The moment was tense and electric, and I knew something awful was about to happen.

Suddenly, the dinosaur the man was photographing reared his head back. He pointed his snout to the sky and let out an unbelievable, savage roar.

The crowd, thinking it was all part of the show, applauded. They clapped and cheered . . . until the gigantic dinosaur leaned forward, opened its mouth, and took the shocked photographer into his powerful jaws and lifted him off the ground!

28

Shrieks of horror rang out as the man was pulled from the ground. He dropped his camera, and it went flying into the air, tumbling back to earth. Snared within the powerful jaws of the enormous dinosaur, the poor man began frantically kicking his legs and waving his arms.

People began running everywhere. They finally realized that what was going on wasn't part of the park's show, that something had gone seriously wrong. No one was taking the time to take pictures anymore, as they were more concerned with running away from the herd of dinosaurs.

Behind us, in the parking lot, those who had remained behind were screaming, too. Some were taking pictures. A television news crew had a camera set up, and they were recording video footage for their report.

But the photographer that had been attacked was lucky. For whatever reason, the beast spit him out, luckily pretty close to the ground. He fell to the ground, where he immediately leapt to his feet and began running away.

"I think that guy is the luckiest guy on the planet," Brady said. "Not many people can say they were picked up by a dinosaur, spit back out, and lived to tell about it."

In the parking lot, the scene was complete chaos. People were running for the safety of their cars. Tires squealed as vehicles left. Many people were shouting and screaming.

"At least nobody has been hurt," I said.

"It's only a matter of time," Brady said. "We saw what those dinosaurs can do. We know what they're capable of. That Allosaurus chewed up wood and metal to try to get at us in the restroom. The Tyrannosaurus rex busted through the double doors. They might be mechanical robots, but they're cold-blooded killers."

Then, led by the Tyrannosaurus rex, the herd of dinosaurs began to move. Their motions were slow and deliberate, cautious, and it was like watching elephants moving across the wide, flat plains of the Serengeti.

A chill went through my body as I realized what was happening. Brady and I could only watch, horrified but fascinated, as the gigantic reptiles made their way through the field.

"They've formed a pack," I said. "They've banded together like wolves."

I've heard it said that there is safety in numbers, and it's true. When people—or animals—stick together, the group is stronger than a single individual.

Robots or not, the dinosaurs realized this.

And they were headed straight for the downtown district of Rapid City.

29

We had to do something.

"Come on!" I said, grabbing Brady by his shirt sleeve.

"Where are we going?" he asked.

"Let's find Mr. Putnam," I replied. "I'm sure he knows what's going on, but he might not know that the dinosaurs are headed for the city."

We began running across the parking lot, weaving around frantic, desperate people as they scrambled to get into their vehicles.

"Don't you think that if he could have stopped the dinosaurs by now, he would have?" Brady asked as we sprinted toward the front gate and the box office.

"Your guess is as good as mine," I replied. "But maybe there is something we can do."

The box office was contained in a large lobby area at the front of the park. We entered through glass double doors. People milled about, completely unaware of what had just happened outside in the field.

We darted through the crowd to a counter at the far end of the room. A man and a woman stood behind the desk.

"Sorry," the woman said as we approached them. "There's been a small glitch in the park, and it won't be open for a few hours."

"A small glitch?" Brady asked. "You call what's happened a small glitch? It's not a small glitch . . . it's a catastrophe!"

"We need to see Mr. Putnam," I pleaded.

The man and woman shook their heads.

"I'm sorry," the man said. "Mr. Putnam is a very busy man."

"It will only take a second," I said. "The dinosaurs have gotten loose. They've broken through the wall and are heading for the downtown area."

The man and woman looked stunned. Then, they both broke out into fits of laughter.

"That's funny," the man said.

"It's true!" Brady insisted.

The man and woman continued chuckling.

"You're not going to think it's so funny when you realize that we're not making it up," I said.

Brady was about to say something, but I grabbed him by the shirt sleeve again and pulled him away.

"Come on," I said quietly. "They don't have a clue what's going on. Maybe there's a way we can sneak into the park without them knowing it."

In the lobby, there was a big sign on a wall that read *Park Entrance*. Beneath it was a set of closed double doors painted with colorful dinosaurs. There was a man in a dark blue uniform standing in front of the doors, making sure no one could get through.

"I have an idea," I said. "I'm going to distract him and get his attention. When I do, you run through the doors. I'll try to come with you, but if I don't, don't worry about it. Just get to the command control center and find Mr. Putnam."

"What are you going to do?" Brady asked.

"Don't worry about it," I said. "The guy guarding the doors is looking the other way right now. Stay right here. When you see him move away from the doors, that will be your signal to move. Got it?"

Brady nodded.

"Okay," I said. "Here goes."

I walked away from Brady, thinking to myself: *this whole day just gets crazier and crazier by the minute.*

30

My plan was simple: all I had to do was distract the man and draw him away from the doors, giving Brady time to act.

Instead of walking toward the man guarding the double doors, I walked toward the water fountain about twenty feet away. I leaned over, took a sip of water, and stood back up. Then, I placed the back of my right hand to my forehead, and in a voice loud enough for the man to hear, I spoke.

"Oh my gosh," I said. "I feel like I'm going to faint."

The man guarding the doors suddenly rushed toward me. He looked serious and very concerned.

"Are you okay, Miss?" he said, taking me gently by the arm.

Out of the corner of my eye, I saw Brady move. He ran to the double doors and pushed one of them open.

I didn't respond to the man. Instead, I slipped from his grasp, darted around him, and ran to the open door where Brady waited.

"Hey!" the man yelled. "Stop! You can't go in there!"

But it was too late. Brady and I had already slipped through the doors and into a wide hallway. We had no idea where we were going, but we began running, figuring that we would find our way somehow.

We passed yet another set of double doors

with windows. Through the glass, we saw the wide expanse of the interior of the park: rocks, ancient trees and plants, sand, and even a few lingering dinosaurs that hadn't followed the herd outside. In the distance, we saw the wall of the park reaching up into the sky-painted ceiling.

At the end of the hall was yet another set of double doors with a sign above them that read:

EMPLOYEES ONLY
NO ADMITTANCE

"There," I said, pointing. "The command control center must be back there, somewhere."

We ran to the doors, pushed them open, and ran through. They opened into yet another hallway that looked familiar.

"It's got to be around here somewhere," Brady said.

We came to an intersecting hallway, and stopped.

"Down there!" I said. "I think I remember

walking down this hallway!"

We sprinted down the hall and past the laboratory, knowing we were headed in the right direction. Finally, after going through yet another set of double doors, we reached our destination.

"There it is!" Brady said, pointing to a door ahead of us. "There's the command control center!"

31

We ran to the door, pushed it open, and burst through.

Inside, men and women were busy working at computers, talking loudly and frantically. Mr. Putnam stood in the middle of the room, watching the large monitors on the wall. One of the screens showed activity within the park, where several dinosaurs milled about. Another screen zeroed in on the enormous double doors and the damage that had been done when the Tyrannosaurus rex broke through them.

"Mr. Putnam!" I said loudly.

Mr. Putnam turned, shocked to see us standing in the room. Then, his look of surprise turned to an expression of great relief, and he raised his arms wide.

"You're alive!" he said.

"We're fine," I said.

"We tried to get the rescue squad to you," he explained, walking toward us. "But it was too dangerous. There was nothing we could do without putting even more people in danger."

"What happened?" Brady asked. "Why are the dinosaurs acting that way?"

"A computer virus," Mr. Putnam explained. "Somehow, our mainframe computer network was infected with a virus. It affected the programming software that controls the dinosaurs. We've been working to try to fix it, and I think we're close."

"Can't you just shut them off?" I asked.

Mr. Putnam shook his head. "The computer

172

virus has completely eliminated our control, including our ability to turn off the dinosaurs. Until we can eradicate the virus, we can't stop them."

"*What does 'eradicate' mean?*" Brady whispered into my ear.

"*It means to get rid of something,*" I whispered back.

"*Gotcha,*" Brady said quietly.

"A bunch of dinosaurs are heading toward the city," I said.

Mr. Putnam nodded. "We watched them break down the double doors," he said. "We've been following them on our monitors."

He pointed to a large, flat screen television in the corner of the room, where we could see the herd of dinosaurs approaching the city.

"We've alerted the police," Mr. Putnam continued, "and they are trying to evacuate the city right now. But if the dinosaurs reach the downtown area, they'll do a terrible amount of damage. We are trying to stop them before they get there."

A man seated at a computer turned. "Making another attempt, sir," he said.

Mr. Putnam walked to where the man sat and stood behind him, looking at the computer screen. It displayed nothing but a series of letters and numbers and symbols, a bunch of gobbledygook computer language that I didn't understand.

"Keep your fingers crossed," Mr. Putnam said. "If this doesn't work, the dinosaurs are going to make it to the city."

The man in front of Mr. Putnam tapped furiously at the computer keyboard. Everyone in the room stared anxiously at the television screen in the far corner, watching the herd of dinosaurs as they neared downtown. The room went silent, except for the tick-tack clicking of the computer keyboard.

The man seated at his computer shook his head. "I'm sorry, sir," he said. "No luck. Nothing seems to work."

Mr. Putnam looked grave. He drew a long

breath, then slowly let it out. "Get the police chief on the phone again," he said. "Tell him the bad news. Rapid City is going to be destroyed."

32

A stunned silence fell over the room. You could have heard a pin drop as we watched the dinosaurs on the television screen. The herd had spread out, and some of the dinosaurs had reached the outskirts of the city.

Police cars began to arrive with their lights flashing. They surrounded the herd in an attempt to form a barrier with their vehicles.

It did nothing to stop the dinosaurs, who

simply stepped on top of the cars, crushing them easily. Police officers had to scramble from their vehicles and run to safety.

"Nothing's going to stop them," Brady said. "Those things are going to demolish Rapid City. Everything is going to be destroyed."

Suddenly, the man seated in front of Mr. Putnam spoke.

"Hang on, hang on!" he said. "I think I've got it! I think I can override the virus!"

"Hurry!" Mr. Putnam said.

The man seated at the computer worked furiously at the keyboard, making sounds like popping popcorn.

"There!" he said triumphantly. "I think that did it!"

Eyes remained glued to the television screen in the corner.

"They stopped!" someone said. "None of them are moving! It's like they're frozen in place!"

A woman pointed to yet another television screen on the wall.

"The ones in the park have stopped, too."

We glanced at the screen and looked at the park scene. I counted five dinosaurs, and all were as still as shadows.

A cheer rose up within the room. Several people hugged each other, and many of them shook Mr. Putnam's hand. He smiled, and the relief showed in his face.

Rapid City was safe.

33

Three months later:

We were kind of famous for a while, as both Brady and I were interviewed on television. Our friends talked about us at school, and some guy who writes a series of scary books said he wanted to write a story about what had happened to us in the park. He seemed like a nice guy, but he wore really freaky googly glasses that made his eyeballs look like they were popping out.

Once again, we had been invited to attend the grand opening of Putnam's Dinosaur Park when it was rescheduled to open in late July. It had been closed ever since the chaotic events of April 24th, until everything had been repaired, including the computers. Mr. Putnam wanted to be certain that something like that would never, ever happen again.

And, again, Brady and I had been invited to be the first two visitors to the park.

Were we nervous? No. Mr. Putnam had given us another tour, showing us what had gone wrong with the computers, and why. Then, he took us through the park. This time, the dinosaurs behaved perfectly. It was really cool to see them up close without having to worry about them coming after us.

After the tour, Mr. Putnam left us on our own while he greeted visitors entering the park. Soon, hundreds of people were milling about, smiling and laughing, taking pictures, and having a great time.

Brady and I were going to eat lunch at the *Jurassic Café,* but it was too crowded. We decided to wait a while, so we went into the souvenir shop. Mr. Putnam had given us each a $50 gift certificate, so we bought T-shirts, books, a dinosaur video, and some postcards. I bought a stuffed dinosaur for my little brother. Even though he wasn't all that into dinosaurs, I knew he would love the gift.

"This place is so cool," Brady said. "Now that I know we're not going to be eaten by a giant Tyrannosaurus rex or an Allosaurus or some other dinosaur, it's a lot of fun."

"I can't wait to come back," I said. "I don't think I'll ever get tired of this place."

Carrying our bags of souvenirs, we left the shop and walked into the lobby. There was a line of people waiting to get into the park. Standing nearby was a boy I thought I recognized. I walked up to him and was about to say 'hello,' but when he turned, I realized he wasn't the person I thought he was.

He looked at me expectantly.

"I'm sorry," I said. "I thought you were someone I knew. He has brown hair and is the exact same height you are."

The boy shook his head. "I'm not from around here," he said. "I don't know anybody except my grandparents who live here in Rapid City."

"Where are you from?" Brady asked.

"Massachusetts," he said.

"Massachusetts?!?!" I said. "That's a long ways away."

"I come here every summer and spend two weeks with my grandparents," the boy said. "I'm Damon Lewis."

"I'm Autumn McLachlan," I said, "and this is my friend, Brady Vanguard."

"Have you guys been in the park, yet?" Damon asked.

I looked at Brady and smiled. Then, I looked back at Damon and spoke.

"Yeah," I said. "In more ways than you can

imagine." Brady and I told Damon about what had happened to us back in April, and he listened, wide-eyed.

"Wow," he said, after we'd finished. "That's crazy."

"It sure was," I said. "In fact, there's some author who's going to write a scary book about what happened to us."

Damon frowned. "He should write a book about what happened to me and my friends last month."

"Why?" Brady asked. "What happened to you last month?"

Damon shook his head. "I've already been over this with a bunch of people," he replied. "There's not a single person who believes me. Except, of course, the friends who were with me. But no one believes them, either."

"You're talking to two kids who were attacked by dinosaurs," I said. "We know crazy things can happen."

"Yeah," Brady said. "So, tell us what

happened."

"Okay," Damon said. "I'll just say one word, and see if you laugh at me."

"Go for it," I said.

"All right," Damon replied. "Martians."

I looked at Brady, and he looked at me.

"Like, little green men from outer space?" I asked.

Damon shook his head. "They're definitely not little, and they aren't green, either."

"You're right," Brady said. "I don't believe that for a minute. But I'd still like to hear what happened."

"Yeah," I chimed in. "Me, too."

"Okay," Damon said, "but I'm a little hungry. Is there a place to get a bite to eat around here?"

I pointed. "There's the *Jurassic Café,* right over there," I said. "We were just waiting for the crowd to thin out, so we could grab some lunch. Why don't you join us, and you can tell us about the Martians."

So, that's how we met Damon Lewis, and

how we came to hear all about the Martians that had crash landed their spacecraft in Massachusetts. To this day, I'm not sure if I believe him, but he sure told a fascinating story . . . .

Next:

#35: Maniac Martians Marooned in Massachusetts

Continue on for a FREE preview!

I

What I'm going to tell you is a story about Martians.

That's right.

Alien beings from Mars, one of the closest planets to Earth.

Now, you might think that this is a science fiction story, and that's partially true.

But, for the most part, it's a horror story. A nightmare in real life, a terrifying experience that nearly cost the lives of me and my friends one awful summer in Massachusetts.

But I'll also say this: if we hadn't stopped the Martians, they might have gone on to take over the entire state, then the country, and, quite possibly, the world.

So, you might say that we're heroes, and that alone makes me feel kind of proud. Oh, no one knows we're heroes, and we don't care. We're just glad that we did what we did, that we acted in time to save ourselves . . . let alone the entire human race.

My name is Damon Lewis, and I live in Boston, Massachusetts. I am 11 years old, and in the fifth grade. I have a sister, named Tracy, and she is one year younger than me. She is in the fourth grade. We get along fairly well, for the most part.

And up until one particular vacation last summer, I would have to say that my life was relatively boring. That's not to say that I don't have any fun. I have some great friends, and I love lots of things like sports, video games, and being outdoors. I think I like many of the things most kids my age do.

And one thing I look forward to every year is our family vacation. Each year, we go somewhere different. One year we went to Disney World in Florida, and it was awesome! Another year, we went to Cedar Point in Ohio, and that was a lot of fun, too.

However, last summer, we decided to stay in our home state of Massachusetts, and explore some of the places that we hadn't yet been to.

One of those places is called October Mountain Forest. It is on the eastern side of Massachusetts, and about a two and a half hour drive from our home in Boston. Dad told me all about it one morning during breakfast.

"You'll love it, Damon," he said to me as he placed his cup of coffee on the table. He had a map spread out before him, and he pointed to a particular spot with his index finger. "It's the biggest State Forest in Massachusetts, and there are miles and miles of hiking trails. You and Tracy are going to have the time of your lives."

And, for the most part, my dad was right: Tracy and I, along with a friend that we met at the campsite, Amber Duncan, would have the time of our lives. We just didn't know that having the time of our lives would also lead to an incredible discovery . . . and the most terrifying day we'd ever experienced.

On the day we left for vacation, we got a late start because Dad couldn't find the car keys. He and Mom hunted all over for them. He was getting pretty angry, too. Dad gets mad when he loses things. One time, he forgot where he placed his wallet and he tore the house upside down looking for it. Of course, his wallet was in the exact place where he'd left it: on the seat of the car in the garage. Still, he claimed he hadn't left it there, and thought that someone else must've taken it to the car on purpose. Crazy.

Anyway, after about an hour of searching for the keys, guess what? Dad found them right where he had left them. They were on the mantle over the fireplace. I had no idea why he'd put them there, but being that he was the last one that had driven the car, he was most obviously the one who had placed them there.

Our drive was going to take us a couple of hours. For the most part, it was uneventful. I played a video game while Tracy read a book. We got into an argument about something, and my dad, who was still angry from getting a late start, got mad at us.

"Do you want me to turn this car around?" he said as he looked up at the rearview mirror. Tracy had just slapped me in the shoulder, and I slapped her shoulder in return.

"Because I will," Dad continued. "Don't make me turn this car around, because I'll do it in a heartbeat."

The rest of the trip was silent. I didn't pay any attention to Tracy, and she paid no attention to me. I just played my game and caught glimpses of road signs as we traveled on Interstate 90. Once in a while, Mom would say something about our vacation, and how fun it was going to be to stay in a campground instead of a hotel.

I was looking forward to that, too. Sure, I enjoyed staying in hotels when we went on vacation, but it wasn't very often that we went camping. I was looking forward to having a campfire, roasting marshmallows after dark, and helping Dad cook breakfast over the fire in the morning. I'd even bought a new pocket knife at a sporting goods store, and I couldn't wait to use it. There were a lot of things I was looking forward to . . . but getting attacked by Martians wasn't one of them.

I know it sounds crazy and unbelievable, and I wouldn't blame anyone if they didn't believe me.

Still, it happened, and to this day, I feel very lucky to be alive.

It took us longer than expected to get to our campsite, because Dad took a wrong turn and we got lost. Dad said that the road he was taking was a shortcut to the State Forest, but, as it turned out, it took us nearly sixty miles in another direction. We had to go all the way back and get on Interstate 90 again. Dad went on and on about how there 'used to be a shortcut, back in the 'good old days,' that they 'must have changed the route.'

I thought the whole thing was kind of funny, but I didn't say anything. I didn't want him mad at me!

So, by the time we got to October Mountain State Forest, it was already getting dark. And by the time we got around to putting up our tents, the stars were out. Dad and Mom had a large tent where they would sleep, and Tracy and I had a smaller, two-person tent that we set up next to theirs.

There were others in the campground, too. Some people had tents, while others had big recreational vehicles. We could see campfires glowing in the early night, and could smell the crisp, punky odor of wood smoke.

And I must admit: I really was excited. The last time we had used the tent, I'd set it up in our backyard. I had a friend over and we stayed up really late, telling ghost stories.

But that really wasn't camping. Now, we were a long ways from home in a place we'd never been before. I was excited about exploring the area and seeing some new things.

The next morning, Dad was in a much better

mood. He was making breakfast over an open fire, and I awoke to the fantastic smells of scrambled eggs and bacon. The sun was already up, and it was a beautiful morning. I dressed, found my pocket knife, stuffed it into my pocket, and went outside into the fresh, cool morning air.

After breakfast, Dad sent me on an errand.

"Damon?" he said. He was holding an empty plastic gallon water jug in each hand.

"Yeah?"

"Will you take these over to the water spigot and fill them up?" he asked.

"Sure," I replied. I dried off my hands, took the water jugs from Dad, and set out across a small field, winding around other campsites, making my way toward a couple of small restrooms. Near the restrooms was a watering station, and there was a girl about my age doing the same thing I was about to do: filling up jugs of water. When she saw me coming, she smiled.

"I'll be done in just a second," she said as I approached. "Actually, I've been going slow, because I know that as soon as I get back to our campsite, my parents are going to put me to work again. I'm trying to kill some time."

I put the empty jugs on the ground. "Take your time," I replied. "I'm in no rush." Then, I looked around. "It sure is a nice day," I said.

The girl looked up and around. "It sure is," she said. "There's not a single cloud in the sky, and it looks like it's going to be—"

She halted her sentence abruptly. Not only that, but her jaw fell and her eyes widened. She dropped the jug of water that she had been filling and pointed up into the sky, her face filled with fear and alarm.

"Look at that!" she shouted. *"What in the world is that?!?!"*

ABOUT THE AUTHOR

Johnathan Rand has been called 'one of the most prolific authors of the century.' He has authored more than 75 books since the year 2000, with well over 4 million copies in print. His series include the incredibly popular **AMERICAN CHILLERS, MICHIGAN CHILLERS, FREDDIE FERNORTNER, FEARLESS FIRST GRADER,** and **THE ADVENTURE CLUB.** He's also co-authored a novel for teens (with Christopher Knight) entitled **PANDEMIA.** When not traveling, Rand lives in northern Michigan with his wife and three dogs. He is also the only author in the world to have a store that sells only his works: **CHILLERMANIA!** is located in Indian River, Michigan and is open year round. Johnathan Rand is not always at the store, but he has been known to drop by frequently. Find out more at:

www.americanchillers.com

Join the official

AMERICAN

CHILLERS

FAN CLUB!

Visit www.americanchillers.com for details!

Johnathan Rand travels internationally for school visits and book signings! For booking information, call:

1 (231) 238-0338!

www.americanchillers.com

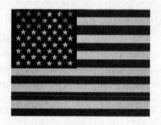